Maizie Albright
Star Detective

★ ★ ★ ★

20
CARATS

★ ★ ★ ★

Wall Street Journal bestselling author
Larissa Reinhart

PRAISE FOR LARISSA REINHART

THE FINLEY GOODHART CRIME CAPER SERIES

"This is as fun a novel as it is moving and at times heart-breaking, never the more so when the final page comes and readers are only left wanting more."

CYNTHIA CHOW, *KING'S RIVER LIFE MAGAZINE* ON THE CUPID CAPER

"Another great mystery by Larissa Reinhart. Con artists, murder, a cast of sinister characters, and some laughs along the way. Loved it."

TERRI L. AUSTIN, AUTHOR OF THE *ROSE STRICKLAND MYSTERIES* ON THE CUPID CAPER

THE MAIZIE ALBRIGHT STAR DETECTIVE SERIES

"Fun characters, a perfect setting, and a mystery that will keep you guessing until the end, this book truly has it all!"

SHANNON VANBERGEN, USA TODAY BESTSELLING AUTHOR OF THE GLOCK GRANNIES MYSTERIES ON 20 CARATS

"Fans of humorous mysteries like Janet Evanovich's Stephanie Plum, and Elle Cosimano's Finlay Donovan should pick up this series. We all need some fun in our reading lives!"

"I loved this very fun romance mystery novel. Five out of five stars."

"I love the characters in this series, they're what keeps me coming back. If you're looking for a fun series that will keep you turning the pages, you've found it here."

"I highly recommend this series and definitely start with Book 1 you won't be sorry!!! Well written characters and a great mystery. I cannot wait to see what happens next!"

"The perfect combination of mystery, romance, and laughs."

"18 Caliber was my first Maizie Albright Star Detective Mystery--I'm hoping it won't be my last. This was a fun read--a fast-paced caper that kept me entertained until the end."

"The mystery and detective cases drive the story, but Larissa Reinhart's characters steal the show every time."

"NC-17 is simply fabulous. Fans of cozy mysteries, southern chick lit, hick lit, crime capers, and humorous mysteries will love it."

"If you love southern settings with plenty of sweet tea and eccentric characters, the meet up of these two heroines is epic."

"Maizie's missteps make each of her successes an absolute joy, and I encourage readers to delve into this lively, funny, and genuinely satisfying series."

"With visually descriptive narrative, humorous quips, witty repartee and a quirky cast of characters, this was a such a fun book to read."

"Larissa writes a delightful book. Suspense, romance, and some funny situations. [Maizie's] a teen star grown up to new possibilities."

"I love Larissa Reinhart's books because they are funny but they also show the big heart of the protagonist."

"Hollywood glitz meets backwoods grit in this fast-paced ride on D-list celeb Maizie Albright's waning star. Sassy, sexy, and fun, 15 Minutes is hours of enjoyment—and a wonderful start to a fun new series from the charmingly Southern-fried Reinhart."

"Maizie Albright is the kind of fresh, fun, and feisty 'star detective' I love spending time with, a kind of Nancy Drew meets Lucy Ricardo. Move over, Janet Evanovich. Reinhart is my new "star mystery writer!"

"Child star and hilarious hot mess Maizie Albright trades Hollywood for the backwoods of Georgia and pure delight ensues. Maizie's my new favorite escape from reality."

THE CHERRY TUCKER MYSTERY SERIES

"Anytime artist Cherry Tucker has what she calls a Matlock moment, can investigating a murder be far behind? A Composition in Murder is a rollicking good time."

"This is a winning series that continues to grow stronger and never fails to entertain with laughs, a little snark, and a ton of heart."

KINGS RIVER LIFE MAGAZINE ON A COMPOSITION IN MURDER

"Cherry Tucker is a strong, sassy, Southern sleuth who keeps you on the edge of your seat."

TONYA KAPPES, *USA TODAY* BESTSELLING AUTHOR ON THE BODY IN THE LANDSCAPE

"Because of Cherry's experiences, she knows that —Super Swine notwithstanding—man has always been the most dangerous game, making her the perfect protagonist for this giggle-inducing, down-home fun."

BETTY WEBB, *MYSTERY SCENE MAGAZINE* ON THE BODY IN THE LANDSCAPE

"The perfect blend of funny, intriguing, and sexy! Another must-read masterpiece from the hilarious Cherry Tucker Mystery Series."

– ANN CHARLES, *USA TODAY* BESTSELLING AUTHOR OF THE *DEADWOOD* AND *JACKRABBIT JUNCTION MYSTERY SERIES* ON DEATH IN PERSPECTIVE

"Artist and accidental detective Cherry Tucker goes back to high school and finds plenty of trouble and skeletons...Reinhart's charming, sweet-tea flavored series keeps getting better!"

GRETCHEN ARCHER, *USA TODAY* BESTSELLING AUTHOR OF THE *DAVIS WAY CRIME CAPER SERIES* ON DEATH IN PERSPECTIVE

"Like front-porch lemonade, Reinhart's cast of characters offer a perfect balance of tart and sweet."

SOPHIE LITTLEFIELD, BESTSELLING AUTHOR OF *A BAD DAY FOR SORRY* ON HIJACK IN ABSTRACT

"Reinhart manages to braid a complicated plot into a tight and funny tale. The reader grows to love Cherry and her quirky worldview, her sometimes misguided judgment, and the eccentric characters that populate the country of Halo, Georgia. Cozy fans will love this latest Cherry Tucker mystery."

MARY MARKS, *NEW YORK JOURNAL OF BOOKS* ON HIJACK IN ABSTRACT

"Reinhart's country-fried mystery is as much fun as a ride on the tilt-a-whirl at a state fair. Readers who like a little small-town charm with their mysteries will enjoy Reinhart's series."

DENISE SWANSON, *NEW YORK TIMES* BESTSELLING AUTHOR OF THE *SCUMBLE RIVER MYSTERIES* ON STILL LIFE IN BRUNSWICK STEW

"This mystery keeps you laughing and guessing from the first page to the last. A whole-hearted five stars."

"*Portrait of a Dead Guy* is an entertaining mystery full of quirky characters and solid plotting...Highly recommended for anyone who likes their mysteries strong and their mint juleps stronger!"

"Reinhart is a truly talented author and this book was one of the best cozy mysteries we reviewed this year."

"It takes a rare talent to successfully portray a beer-and-hormone-addled artist as a sympathetic and worthy heroine, but Reinhart pulls it off with tongue-in-cheek panache. Cherry is a lovable riot, whether drooling over the town's hunky males, defending her dysfunctional family's honor, or snooping around murder scenes."

CONTENTS

20 CARATS, Maizie Albright Star Detective #9

Print ISBN: 978-1-7377550-3-6

eBook ISBN: 979-82151008-8-2

Library of Congress Control Number: 2023915355

Original cover design by James of GoOnWrite

https://www.goonwrite.com/

Past Perfect Press

Printed in the USA

Author photo by Scott Asano

BOOKS BY LARISSA REINHART

MAIZIE ALBRIGHT STAR DETECTIVE SERIES (IN ORDER)

15 MINUTES

16 MILLIMETERS

NC-17

A VIEW TO A CHILL

17.5 CARTRIDGES IN A PEAR TREE

18 CALIBER

18 1/2 DISGUISES

19 CRIMINALS

20 CARATS

21 GUNS

A CHERRY TUCKER MYSTERY SERIES (IN ORDER)

A CHRISTMAS QUICK SKETCH (prequel)

PORTRAIT OF A DEAD GUY

STILL LIFE IN BRUNSWICK STEW

HIJACK IN ABSTRACT

THE VIGILANTE VIGNETTE

DEATH IN PERSPECTIVE

THE BODY IN THE LANDSCAPE

A VIEW TO A CHILL

A COMPOSITION IN MURDER

A MOTHERLODE OF TROUBLE

A FINLEY GOODHART CRIME CAPER SERIES

THE PIG'N A POKE

A Finley Goodhart Crime Caper prequel

"It's sassy, sexy, and southern suspense at its best."

DEBORAH DELANEY
BOOK BUYSEWS

THE
PIG'N
A POKE

A FINLEY GOODHART
CRIME CAPER SHORT

LARISSA REINHART
Wall Street Journal Bestselling Author

When a winter storm traps ex-con Finley at the Pig'N a Poke roadhouse, she finds her criminal past useful in solving a murder.

Free for my VIP Readers!

Join Larissa's email group where she shares exclusive content, news, and giveaways — **www.larissareinhart.com/larissasreaders** — and receive *The Pig'n A Poke* as a gift.

Note: Larissa will not share your email address and you can unsubscribe at any time.

20 CARATS

A MAIZIE ALBRIGHT "BETWEEN CASES"
ROMANTIC-COMEDY MYSTERY NOVELLA

MAIZIE ALBRIGHT STAR DETECTIVE
BOOK 9

LARISSA REINHART

Past Perfect Press

ACKNOWLEDGMENTS

A big thanks to Tonya Kappes and Rachel Brown for all their work on Twisty Tales & Cozy Crimes. Thanks so much for the invitation to join this fun group of wonderful writers and for giving me the excuse to add another Maizie Albright!

I'm grateful to my family for tip-toeing around me in the morning, so I can get in a few paragraphs before work every day.

As always, a huge thanks to Ritter Ames, my friend and an incredible editor. I appreciate the time you took out of your busy schedule for me and Maizie. (A year later, I am crushed by your absence and I miss you.)

And my belated gratitude to my critique partner, Terri L. Austin. 20 Carats is the only story you haven't read before publication. I will still continue to write with you in mind, trying to make you laugh. I miss you!

For Terri
I miss trying to make you laugh.
For Ritter
I miss trying to make you laugh, too.
Writing has been very lonely without the two of you.

ONE
#TIFFANYBLUES

WHEN MY PHONE trilled "I'm Too Sexy," I took my time deciding whether to answer. Hoping that long hesitation would make the decision for me. I was on a stakeout, sitting in the cab of a truck, and there wasn't much happening, but there was always a chance something would soon. In my experience — and with my luck — that chance generally occurred when I was distracted.

It's amazing how many subjects do something during a quick run to a McDonald's for a tee-tee break.

Okay, fine. And a quick fry and pie order. I'm not the kind of person to use a bathroom without ordering something. And sitting in a vehicle watching a motel or whatever makes a person hungry. Plus, in my old career, I wasn't allowed within fifty feet of a McDonald's. Literally. It was in my contracts. Written by my ex-manager and still-mother, Vicki Albright. She knew I had a weakness for fries and pies. Any kind of non-saturated fat, really.

I was Maizie Albright—child actress and teen celebrity—before I became Maizie Albright, apprentice PI. Fries and pies were a big no-no then. Still should be. My eyes were still sea glass-green. My hair, still ginger. But my curves no longer fit into the teen detective cheer skirt.

But that's what leggings are for, right?

Anyway, I knew by the ringer who had called without even checking. Giulio Belloni. My ex-costar from my post-teen reality show, *All Is Albright*. Also, my ex-fiancé. But not an ex-friend. Even though he dumped me when I quit *All Is Albright*. Then gotten engaged to Vicki — the aforementioned ex-manager and still-mother — to advance his career.

She'd done it to advance the ratings.

But still. Ew, right?

They'd both moved on relationship-wise and career-wise (or both in Giulio's case since he'd gotten engaged again in a *Bachelorette*-style spin-off). All's well that ends well and all that, but Giulio wasn't my favorite person at the moment. He also wasn't Wyatt Nash's favorite person. Ever. And Wyatt Nash had joined me on the stakeout. For fun. Another reason not to pick up the phone.

Nash was a real PI. He was also my real...

I can't call a man who looks like he could double for Dwayne Johnson a boyfriend. There's nothing boyish about him. And he wasn't my fiancé. Not yet, anyway. (Fingers crossed!)

"Are you going to answer that?" said Nash without taking his eyes off the storage unit across the street.

"I'm letting it roll over to voicemail," I said. "It's just Giulio."

"What's Baloney want?"

As I said, Giulio Belloni wasn't Nash's favorite person. "I'm not sure. I haven't heard from him in weeks." Immediately I felt guilty. "I should call him back."

Nash glanced at me. "Why didn't you just answer?"

"I didn't want to talk to him."

"Then don't."

Life was that simple for Nash. Life was not that simple for me. I'd rather avoid personal and professional dilemmas. That was something my therapist, Renata, and I had been working on. Before I left California and moved home to Georgia. Technically, Renata wasn't my therapist anymore. But we still had therapy sessions in my head.

Which also sounds better in my head and not aloud, so never mind.

"I haven't spoken to Giulio in a long time. Not since he got engaged to…" I shifted in the cab seat. "I can't even remember her name. That's how bad a friend I've been."

"Or it's because he's been engaged so many times, you've lost track." Nash rolled his eyes. "Why should you feel bad? He could call you."

"He just did."

And according to "I'm Too Sexy" playing from my backpack, Giulio was calling again. This time I answered.

"Darling." Giulio took a long moment to greet me with mock kisses over the phone. Giulio had been a soap star in Italy before getting the dream role as Maizie Albright's fiancé and taking the American reality TV world by storm. He still greeted like an Italian *telenovele* star, though. "You never call me anymore."

"I could say the same," I said, taking a page from Nash.

"So busy, darling." His shrug projected through the phone line. "But I am calling you now. I tried just a moment ago. You were busy, too, yes?"

"I'm on a stakeout."

"How exciting, darling. I'd love to join you on a stakeout. I can picture it now. We sit in a Ferrari beneath the single streetlight on a dark street."

"That's a very bad idea for a stakeout," I said. "Ferraris tend to stand out. And the streetlight will shine a spotlight on what we're doing."

Nash raised an eyebrow, gave a humph of disgust, and turned his attention back to the storage units.

"Okay, okay. Alfa Romeo," continued Giulio. "I peer through the *binoculare*. You are curled up beside me, the camera with the long lens in your hand. However, your eyes are not on the subject. They are on me. I am thinking about catching our suspect. But you are thinking about—"

"Why did you call?" With Giulio, it was best to get to the point. His imagination tended toward a singular topic. Which made him a terrific soap star. And reality star, for that matter.

"Sorry, darling. It is terrible. I can't believe it. And to think, me? How could they?" He paused. "Don't you think?"

"I have no idea what you're talking about."

"My arrest, darling. You haven't heard? I would've called you to bail me out, but I know you are so poor now." He paused. "It's like I'm back in the *sceneggiati*, no? The lover framed for the crime he didn't commit. The *passione* of jealousy. Or maybe greed. Perhaps wrath."

"What arrest?" I said before Giulio listed more motives for his personal soap opera plot.

He sighed. "They accuse me of burglary."

"Wait. What?" Giulio was a lot of things, but not a thief. "What did they think you stole?"

Nash looked over.

"I don't even know. Some trinket. A gold jewelry box. What do I want with a jewelry box?"

"That is weird."

"It's not even blue, darling. And it's old. You know I am not into the vintage."

"Not blue? What do you mean?"

"They say it's from Tiffany's. I always get the blue box when I buy from Tiffany's. The women like Tiffany Blue, no? And gold?" He scoffed. "It's the sterling silver the women want. And diamonds."

At "diamonds," he sighed with all the Latin ennui he could muster. "These women, Maizie, will make me broke with all their want of diamonds. You were good that way, my dear. I could get by with a nice dinner.

Bribe you with the dessert, eh?" He laughed, but there wasn't any genuine mirth to it.

I cocked my head, ignoring his bluster. I knew of a vintage Tiffany's box. 20-carat gold. Cedar-lined. It wasn't stolen, but some treachery had been involved in purchasing that box.

"More importantly," I said. "Why do the police accuse you of stealing this jewelry box?"

Nash's Paul Newman-blue eyes had narrowed and the little scar on his chin had whitened with his jaw clenching. A bloop-bleep of a car alarm sounded, but Nash's focus remained on me.

"Bah, police," Giulio began.

"Get to the point," I interrupted. "This is important."

"Of course, it's important," he snapped. "It is me they are accusing of stealing. They found the gold box in my chalet."

My breath caught. Nash laid a comforting hand on my thigh. I placed a hand on top of his. "Did they have a warrant to search your house?"

"*Sì, sì.* But why? I let them in when they asked. What is with the paperwork?"

Paperwork? My chest tightened and my stomach clenched. "Does this box have an inscription?"

"I don't know. I tell you, I didn't take this box. I don't even know this box. It is all *ridicolo*…"

I put the phone on speaker and laid it in my lap to wait out the litany of Latin obscenities. Giulio would need a minute, which I used for relating his story to Nash. "This is bad. They had a warrant to search his house. The jewelry box must have been reported stolen and someone pointed the police toward Giulio."

Nash grimaced. "Did it have jewelry in it?"

"He didn't say. But if it's the box I'm thinking of, it doesn't need jewelry. It's valuable."

"Stealing an empty jewelry box does seem odd, even for Giulio."

"The only thing Giulio ever steals is the spotlight."

"If I stole the spotlight from you, I am sorry, but I can't help it if the camera loves me. You know this," said Giulio. "Now please go to your *polizia* friend and tell him I'm innocent. If you must seduce the policeman to convince him, so be it. Whatever must be done for justice, no?"

Seeing the look on Nash's face, I regretted putting Giulio on speakerphone. "I'm happy to *talk* to Detective Mowry and learn what I can. But before I go, Giulio, do you know whose box it was? Who accused you?"

"No! Why do I have the enemy? Who would want to hurt Giulio?"

I imagined a lot of broken hearts lay between Georgia and Italy via California. Some of these women might want to hurt Giulio. But I had more than an inkling I knew the owner of the box. If I was right, falsely accusing Giulio didn't make sense. There had to be some kind of miscommunication.

"I'm sure we'll get this cleared up for you. Don't worry. As long as you didn't do anything wrong…"

"*Certo che no!* I swear to you, Maizie, I have never seen this box before. I have been framed, I tell you. This horrible box was planted in the chalet by my enemy."

"And when was the last time you spoke to Vicki?"

TWO

#BELLONIBOMBSHELL

"THIS DOESN'T MAKE ANY SENSE," I said to Nash.

While I'd tried (and failed) to get more information from Giulio, Nash had turned back to watch the storage unit. More of nothing continued to happen there. But I now had Giulio's arrest to entertain me.

"Who are you going to call first — Vicki or Mowry?" Nash's attention remained on the building, but I felt him checking me from the corner of his eye.

"I know how to confirm if the jewelry box is Vicki's by the description, so Ian's probably best." Black Pine police detective Ian Mowry was our go-to for help with local crime.

"Good. Better to have your facts in order before attempting a conversation with Vicki."

That was true, but I sighed anyway. In the past, Vicki had made some ethically questionable decisions. Mainly to advance my career (and hers through mine). But there was always an end to her means. Accusing Giulio of stealing her vintage Tiffany's jewelry box? I couldn't see the point.

"I'm sure you're right about this being some kind of miscommunication." Nash patted my shoulder. Awkwardly. He wasn't much of a patter, but he meant well.

"A miscommunication that landed Vicki's expensive box in Giulio's bachelor pad."

"Maybe Vicki left it there when they were pretend-dating."

"Wasn't Giulio still at the resort during that charade? I thought he just moved to the mountain recently."

"The movers could have unpacked it without Giulio knowing. It's not like Giulio's interested in interior design. He's also not observant unless there's a mirror involved."

Nash nodded. Then shook his head. "Still doesn't explain why Vicki would have him arrested."

I sighed again. At the best of times, talking to Vicki was challenging. This wasn't close to the best of times. More like the worst. I called Ian.

"Hey honey," Ian drawled. "Good to hear from you. We haven't had lunch in forever. Are you free this week?"

Ian and I had a lot in common. We loved food and true crime podcasts. Usually at the same time. We had dated for a minute, but my heart hadn't been in it. Mainly because my heart had fixed on Nash and didn't want to give him up. Fortunately, Ian and I remained friends. He was also friends with Nash. It was all good.

Although sometimes the teensiest bit awkward. Like now.

"I would love that, Ian," I said, flashing a look at Nash. He'd given up on watching the storage unit to watch me. "By the way, I've got you on speaker. I'm on a stakeout. With Nash. He joined me for fun."

"Hey Nash, care to have lunch with us?"

Nash snorted. Ian knew Nash wasn't into lunch the way Ian and I were into lunch. Nash saw food as something that kept you alive. Ian and I saw food as something to live for.

"What kind of stakeout?" continued Ian.

"Rowdy's Storage on Sugarberry. Some equipment

was stolen from Black Pine Studio. They think it's an inside job."

"The studio didn't call us?"

"They preferred to keep this quiet. If we find anything, they'll decide whether to press charges or not."

I piped up before Ian had time to decide whether he should be offended. "Ian, Giulio called me—"

"Now, honey, I know you're upset. I understand. We're looking into it."

"You had a warrant to search his house, Ian. That sounds pretty significant."

"We found the stolen piece in his house. That's significant, too." Ian paused. "This started in California. The warrant's from there, not signed here. Before you defend him to the death, how well do you really know Giulio?"

"I was engaged to him."

"I thought that was some kind of publicity stunt. Like his deal with Vicki. And that reality show. Whatever happened to that bachelorette girl?"

"They broke up, I guess. People are allowed to break their engagements, you know. I've been engaged four times myself. And every one of those was real to me. Including Giulio."

"Honey," said Ian gently. "That's the point I'm trying to make. You thought you were engaged to him. He thought differently. Has Giulio told you much about his past?"

"I know what you're doing, Ian. I'm not going to give you details about Giulio's life to further your investigation. This has to do with Vicki. I know the jewelry box is hers."

"Did Giulio tell you that?"

"He didn't know anything about the box. Only that it's gold and vintage. He'd never seen it before." I tempered my rising voice, hating having to defend one friend to another. "As soon as he described it to me, I knew it was Vicki's. If you flip it over, there's an inscribed plaque that says, 'To M, Love J.'"

"Did Giulio tell you about the plaque?"

"Please, Ian. Giulio has no clue. As usual. This is a mix-up. I'm going to talk to Vicki next."

"That's going to be a problem."

"Have you arrested her, too?"

"Hard to do that when Vicki's skiing in Patagonia. Wherever that is." Ian blew out a long breath. "I know this is upsetting news. There's a Montecito Police detective in Black Pine who's tying up the investigation. I read the incident report. It's cut and dry. Vicki discovered the box missing after Giulio's last visit. The detective interviewed her staff and checked her security. Sounds like he did a thorough job before getting the warrant to search Giulio's home."

"I can't believe Vicki would have Giulio arrested."

"It sounds like she's pretty attached to that jewelry box."

She was. But still.

"Do you know what the box is worth, Maizie?" Ian spoke firmly.

"Only its estimated value."

"Around one hundred thousand dollars, although there are bidders who would pay a lot more, I'm told. She insured it for a quarter million."

"Vicki bought it for thirty thousand as a steal. The price dropped significantly when the real origination story came out. Interested parties backed out. The owners and auction company lost money. A lot of people were angry about how she got that box, Ian."

"What do you mean?"

"That box was part of Marilyn Monroe's estate. The inscription initial 'J' was believed to stand for Joe. As in Joe DiMaggio. Vicki proved Jane Russell had given Marilyn that box, not Joe. But Vicki waited until just before the auction to have that bit of information revealed to drive the price down. Disgruntled collectors were leaving threats on her voicemail for weeks after, feeling she hadn't played fair."

"Fair or not, it's a pricey box."

"True. There have been attempts to steal that box in the past. To think that Giulio would just waltz in and steal it, then bring it back to his house in Georgia is ludicrous," I said. "If it was stolen, that Montecito detective has more canvassing to do. In California, not Black Pine."

"Except the box was found in Giulio's home and Vicki hadn't given it to him."

"A misunderstanding, I'm sure."

"Giulio's done this before, Maizie. Ask him about his priors, then we'll talk again."

Shizzles.

THREE

"WHO BUYS a box for thirty thousand dollars?" said Nash. "I don't get it."

"That's not the point," I said. Again. We'd left our stakeout in town to drive up Black Pine Mountain. The tonier homes of Black Pine had mountain views. Vicki's Peanut Mansion had the best view, but Giulio's home had a good one, too. A new build Giulio called a chalet. Its slightly pitched roof had floor-to-ceiling windows facing a wrap-around deck that overhung the mountain slope.

We could see Giulio, waiting on the deck as we drove up. We exited the Silverado beneath him.

"Darling," he called, hanging over the sleek deck rails.

Nash and I halted our trudge up the steep walk from the driveway to look up. I waved. Unnecessarily.

On the deck, Giulio greeted me with double-cheek kisses. "I knew you would come. And you brought your private dick, how delightful."

Behind me, Nash growled.

"What? Did I get my English wrong?" Giulio flashed a look of regret that didn't fool anyone. "*Mi dispiace.* When I am upset, my English is not so good."

"Cut it out," I said. "You need all the help you can get."

"It's true. Thank you for bringing your large friend. He will be much help to move my furniture. My poor little chalet. The police, those monsters, tore up my home in their phony search and seizure."

"I don't think Black Pine police would plant evidence in your house, Giulio."

"Black Pine Police, bah." Giulio made a rude gesture, then began pacing. "They're just sheep. I don't blame those imbeciles. The detective from California leads them."

"The investigation began in California. Technically, it's his case," said Nash. "Although I'm surprised he came all the way to Georgia and didn't let Black Pine handle it."

"A lot of celebrities and well-to-do live in Montecito," I said.

"You mean if you have money and status, the cops will bend over backward to look like they're playing ball," scoffed Nash.

"I don't even know him, but he hates me," moaned Giulio. "This Detective Carter will stop at nothing until he sees me rot in prison."

"Don't be ridiculous. He's just doing his job," said Nash. "Let's stick to facts. Starting with your prior arrest."

FOR A MOMENT, Giulio looked stricken. He quickly recovered with an Italian shrug. "I was a kid. I took the Maserati for a how do you say…joy ride? The American police are digging up my juvenile records from Italy? It's excessive, no?"

"You stole a Maserati?" I said.

"Of course," said Giulio. "Why would an Italian boy take anything but a Maserati? Unless it's Lamborghini. Ferrari. Maybe Ducati. Do you think I would take a little Fiat for a spin? We all did it. Just a boyish prank. I did the community service. It's all forgotten."

"Maybe forgotten by you," said Nash. "But grand theft auto remains on your juvie record. In the US that would have been sealed, but I guess not in Italy. Detective Carter has been thorough."

"How thorough?" said Giulio, suddenly serious.

"Detective Mowry told us you were in California before the jewelry box was stolen," I said. "You stayed at Vicki's. That doesn't help your case at all. Why didn't you tell me?"

"I know how it looks, Maizie. But I didn't steal this box. What do I want with an old jewelry box?"

"Probably for the same reason anyone would want a box worth one hundred grand," said Nash.

"Why did you bring him, Maizie?" whined Giulio. "Nash is just like the rest. Suspicious of a foreigner."

"Nash's not suspicious of foreigners. He's suspicious of everyone," I said. "Besides, you're not foreign to us. You're only foreign when it's convenient."

Giulio threw his hands up in the air and strode the length of the deck, muttering in Italian.

I turned to Nash. "Let's go inside and look around. Give him time to cool off."

"I heard that, Maizie," called Giulio. "I am a passionate man. I heat up quickly but also cool down fast. I'll go with you."

"Fine," whispered Nash. "But if he gets you in his bedroom and heats up, I get to cool him down."

We entered through the glass door off the deck into the living room. The furniture had been pushed from the walls. The corners of his Turkish rug flipped to expose the bare wood floor beneath. The few books and photos on the built-in shelves were disarranged. Some couch cushions had fallen on the floor.

"This isn't so bad," I said. "In *Julia Pinkerton, Teen Detective*, whenever the police searched a house, they always ripped open the couch cushions and smashed a lot of glass. I never understood why they smashed glass. You can see through it."

"Your TV show was not realistic, no? But of course, you did the best you could as Julia," said Giulio, patting my shoulder.

"We won a Golden Globe," I said. "I won an MTV award. Julia Pinkerton wasn't that bad."

"Still, this is terrible for me," said Giulio. "I feel violated."

"Imagine how the owner of the Maserati felt not finding his car," said Nash.

Giulio shot Nash a look. "The owner left the car running and went into a shop. What did he expect? Besides, the butcher usually takes much time with the order. I thought just a quick spin around the block. Who knew the man would get his *prosciutto* so quickly?"

"Where did they find the jewelry box?" I said more as a segue than real detective work. Giulio could be charming and fun. This was not one of those times. A defensive, upset Giulio made me want to punch him. I couldn't imagine the bodily harm Nash felt like doing.

"The detective found it in the bedroom," said Giulio. "Nash, you push the furniture back. Maizie, come with me to my bedroom. For the investigating, no?"

Nash's scar pulsed against the tightening of his jaw.

"We'll go together," I blurted. "If you were smart, you'd want Nash on this, too."

"If I were smart, I wouldn't have let the police into my house," said Giulio.

Nash shot him a look that told his feelings about Giulio's IQ. But we traipsed (Giulio and I traipsed, Nash trod) past the kitchen, where cabinet doors and drawers stood open, and down a hall to the bedrooms. The master bedroom furniture had the blond wood and a modern feel keeping with the Scandinavian design. Eight-by-ten glossies of Giulio in various TV roles lined one wood-paneled wall.

"It is horrible, no?" said Giulio.

"Yes," I said, imagining myself lying in the bed with twenty Giulios looking down at me.

"I will have to send all my clothes to be cleaned and re-pressed." He stood before a dresser, staring at an open drawer where his t-shirts and shorts had been pushed around. He looked up. "Can I bill the police for the dry cleaning?"

"Probably not."

Nash stood in the doorway, arms folded against his thick chest, letting his eyes tour the room. "Where did they find the box?"

"In my safe in the closet," said Giulio. "Can you imagine?"

"That's where I would put a gold box." Nash strode to the walk-in, wrenched open the door, and moved inside.

I looked at Giulio. "This is really bad. I'm not surprised you were arrested. What did your attorney say?"

"The lawyer also says it looks bad." Giulio's shoulders hunched. "Maizie, what can I do? You have to help me. I'm telling the truth. I didn't put the box in the safe. I'm as surprised as everyone else."

Nash reappeared. "Is the sticker on top of the safe the combination?"

"I easily forget the combination," said Giulio. "I didn't keep anything in the safe, so I left the sticker in my move."

"That's a point in your favor," I said.

"Or the police just think he's an idiot when it comes to safes," said Nash.

"I'm trying to stay positive."

Nash glanced at Giulio. "When was the last time you had anything in your safe?"

"I don't use." Giulio shrugged. "Vicki bought it when we had our little romance. She gave it to me because she didn't trust the hotel safe."

"That's another point in your favor," I said. "Is it possible she left the jewelry box in the safe and forgot it when she returned to California?"

"I have no idea. She said the safe was for contracts. I

believe she didn't want me to read mine when she wasn't around. When we ended the relationship, she left the safe and I left the sticker. In case I want to use it someday."

I pressed my lips together and reminded myself that Vicki was on a journey of self-improvement. Then counted to ten and repeated a mantra about life, love, and mothers given to me by my therapist.

Nash waited for me to finish my Vicki cleansing regime. "There's a script in there now."

"Script?" said Giulio. "What script?"

We crowded into the closet. Giulio took the script from the safe and studied it. "How would it get in my safe? This…" He continued in Italian.

I was not a fan of closets. Or a ranting Giulio. I took the script from his hands and backed out of the closet, leaving Giulio to his Italian tirade.

Nash followed me. "Why is he upset?"

"I'm not sure." I rifled through the script titled *The Red Circle*. Giulio's penciled notes filled the script. "I don't remember Giulio talking about this role. This is very odd."

"Giulio is odd."

"Odder. Vicki must have made some mistake about the Marilyn box. I wouldn't think she would be so cruel to Giulio. I'd thought their breakup was amicable, especially since she's reunited with Kevin."

Keven Yuan had been my trainer on the *Kung Fu Kate* set. He'd been like a father to me during my preteen years when I'd been separated from Daddy. Until recently, I hadn't known Kevin's affection for me had also been tied to his affection for Vicki. Kevin was good for Vicki. It thrilled me to have Kevin back in our lives.

However, I still wrestled with my feelings for my ex-manager / still-mother.

Giulio popped out of the closet and snatched the script from my hands. "This is the insult to all insults."

"Why?" said Nash.

"This would have been my star-making movie." Giulio shook the bound pages at us. "I was to play Vogel, the escaped convict originally played by Gian Maria Volonté. This movie would have launched my career from television to box office."

While Giulio ranted in Italian, Nash raised his brows at me.

"The original movie was French, *Le Cercle Rouge*. From the late sixties, maybe 1970? Anyway, it's about a jewelry heist done by two convicts and a crooked cop. The actual heist is a really famous scene." I cocked my head at Giulio. "There's very little dialogue in the movie."

"Good for Giulio then?" said Nash.

"No dialogue is actually harder for an actor. If he could have pulled it off and the movie had been produced and directed well, Giulio's right. It might have launched his career."

"It didn't get made?"

I shook my head. "I vaguely remember the buzz about the remake. I think it was tanked."

"Tanked by your *madre*. We had Lionsgate interested. Can you imagine?" Giulio threw his hands in the air. "And she blew it by trying to hustle her way into the producers' circle. *Inconcepibile*. The audacity of that woman."

"She's pretty audacious. I'm sorry." I hugged Giulio. "That's in the past. You'll have better opportunities.

"Thank you." He clung to me while I rubbed his back. "It's good to have you here. I knew you'd help me."

"Maizie might not be able to do much," said Nash.

"I'll do everything I can."

"I know you will," wailed Giulio, clinging tighter. "You are a good friend to me, Maizie."

Nash's jaw clenched. "It's not good. You want to let her go so I can explain?"

"*Perdonami*. Her body is so comfortable." Giulio unwrapped himself, stepped away from me, and gave Nash a baleful look. "It means nothing."

"I bet." Nash's glare diminished. "Here's the thing. Not only does it look like you stole the—"

"I did not steal," cried Giulio.

"Looks like you did," continued Nash. "But leaving the script in the safe is even worse."

"I didn't put the script in the safe," shouted Giulio.

"Shizzles, Nash's right," I said. "Once the police realize the story behind this script, they're going to think—"

"What?" snapped Giulio, sounding a lot like Vogel from *Le Cercle Rouge*. "What will these pigs think?"

"If Vicki got that movie scrapped, the script screams motive. Not that the value of the Marilyn box didn't give a powerful motive, anyway. But now they know you have a personal motive to steal the jewelry box."

Giulio stopped ranting and blinked.

"Breaking up with Vicki was already personal." I shook my head and looked at Nash. "But wow, this script…"

"Yep. Nail in your coffin," said Nash, and slapped Giulio on the back.

FOUR
#GENTLEMENPREFERBONDS

AFTER REASSURING Giulio we'd do our best to help him, Nash and I tromped down the path sloping to the drive and climbed into his truck.

"Do you want to go back to the storage units?" said Nash.

"Of course not."

"You're right. This time of day, it's too busy. Better to watch it later tonight."

"No, I mean, I've got to help Giulio. I'm putting him first."

Nash didn't reply.

"You don't think I should help him? Someone framed him."

Nash firmed his lips and kept his eyes on the road.

"You don't think someone framed him?"

"I don't know what to think," he drawled. "Other than, framed or not, Baloney's an idiot."

"I know Giulio. He wouldn't do something like this. It just galls me that someone's trying to make him look guilty."

"They're trying to get him arrested." Nash glanced at me. "There's one little problem with your theory."

I raised an eyebrow.

"Someone had to break into Giulio's house and put the box in his safe."

"Putting the box in the safe is no big deal. The combination is taped to it."

"You're avoiding the question."

"It wasn't a question. You made a statement. But okay, I get it. It's a pretty devious plan. Giulio has a pretty devious enemy."

"Giulio doesn't strike me as the kind of guy to have devious enemies."

Nash was right. Still. "Giulio's an extrovert. People tend to drift in and out of his home. He often has parties. He's not overly concerned with security."

"I got that when I pointed out to him that his alarm hadn't been turned on." Nash strummed his fingers on the steering wheel. Nash's specialty was security. Nothing bothered him more than an ill-used security system.

"He probably doesn't like to bother with the keypad." I half-turned in my seat. "Breaking into Giulio's house isn't the real problem. That's the easiest part."

"Except for getting into a safe with the combination taped to the door. That's pretty easy, too." Nash shook his head. I couldn't tell if he was annoyed or befuddled. Probably both.

"The tricky thing was the thief stealing that script."

"And knowing the relevance of that script to use it."

I lifted a shoulder. "It wouldn't be hard to find out that Vicki blew the deal. Using the script as a weapon to indict Giulio was as obvious as knowing Giulio would leave his house unlocked and the safe open. I don't get why the police didn't take it as evidence."

"Because they found the jewelry box. They're not looking for evidence that Giulio didn't steal it." Nash sighed. "Okay, so if he didn't do it, why's someone out to get an idiot like Giulio?"

"Thank you."

Nash glanced at me. "For what?"

"Believing Giulio."

"I don't believe Giulio." His eyes darkened. "I believe you. You're really something when you get worked up."

I felt myself blush and held back what would have been a foolish grin. "I can work with that."

"You want to work with that back at the office? We have a few minutes."

Yes, I did. But there was also making hay while the sun shined, yada. "Maybe later. I want to talk to Ian again. To see if he can put me in touch with Detective Carter."

Nash peeled his gaze off me to pay attention to the road. "Tell me about Vicki and this box."

"It's yellow gold with a Roman key pattern around the edges. Like I said, there was a bidding war for it. The inscription, 'To M, Love Always, J," is on the bottom. There wasn't any provenance except for the original mark from Tiffany's showing they made it in 1950."

"I didn't know Vicki was a Marilyn Monroe fan."

"She's not. Vicki understands the value of sentimentality. She also has an acquaintance who's a Jane Russell buff. Jane and Marilyn became friends on the set of *Gentleman Prefer Blondes*, the same period that Marilyn was with Joe DiMaggio. The movie was released in 1953. Marilyn and Joe divorced in 1954. According to the Jane Russell guru, the box was given to Marilyn in 1954. He believes after her divorce. And it can't be from Arthur Miller because of the initial."

"Vicki waited to use that information publicly to drive the price down."

"Oh yes. All's fair in bidding wars, she would say. Because of that coup, Vicki's nuts about the box. I guess she took it to California with her. I was surprised she didn't leave it here in Black Pine under lock and key."

"It's not the value or the previous owner or anything else. Just that she won the piece in an underhanded way." He shook his head. "I don't get it."

"Hollywood is very competitive. Why do you think so many celebrities buy sports teams?"

Nash remained silent for a moment. "Giulio knew the box was special to Vicki. Probably knew the approximate worth. But he could have stolen it at any time. Why now?"

"Right? Because Giulio didn't steal it." I sighed. "Why wouldn't Vicki handle this privately? The only reason to go after Giulio like this is to ruin his reputation."

"And put him in prison. Call her tonight."

"I can't. She does this two-week ski trip every year. Deliberately stays at a resort in the Andes that's famous for its inaccessibility. Celebrities vacation there knowing there's no internet or cell service." I shook my head. "Some can't handle it. No Twitter or Instagram, you know? But that just makes it more exclusive and weeds out the wannabes."

"What do you mean? You can't call the hotel?"

"I can call the hotel's main line, but that reaches the base camp. They can send emergency messages to the summit. There's a helicopter that goes up daily. Agents and business managers wouldn't stand for it otherwise."

Nash swung a look at me. "She's camping?"

"Yeah, right." I snorted. "Celebrity chef, full staff, and 1,000-thread count sheets. Fully equipped medical and a private runway. The base lodge sits on Lake Nahuel Huapi. It's beautiful."

"Vicki goes to a mountain resort town to get away from the beautiful mountain resort town she lives in? Her Peanut Mansion looks like a mini Overlook. It's on Black Pine Mountain with a view of Black Pine Lake, for cripe's sake." Nash shook his head. "Tahiti, I would get."

"Tahiti in July? What are you thinking?"

"I'm thinking I don't get this lifestyle."

I bit my lip.

He sighed. "So, when can you get in touch with Vicki?"

"I'll leave a message with Hermosa Montaña. The lodge will get it to her in a day or two. Unless she's blocking messages. I'll check with her assistant. She'll be at the base lodge."

"Unbelievable."

We'd reached Black Pine's original downtown, where the old Nash Security Solutions lived above the Dixie Kreme Donut Shop. Downtown still retained its early resort day charm. A few crumbling turn-of-the-twentieth-century buildings. Some early twentieth in so-so shape, like the Dixie Kreme building. And some new-made-to-look-old twenty-first-century brick fronts, like the new Albright Security Solutions office around the corner.

Black Pine experienced a return-to-glory-days resurgence when a chunk of the California movie industry moved to Georgia for cheaper real estate, easier laws, and tax breaks. The same reasons for the original glory days when carpet baggers and southern industry titans made Black Pine a resort destination in the North Georgia Mountains. Just goes to show you, in American history, taxes have always dominated decision-making. We started with the whole tea in the Boston Harbor thing and haven't looked back.

Nash parked on the street facing the brick building. Above the dark storefront window, the painted Dixie Kreme Donuts signage was now a fading white that appeared almost pink. The red neon "Hot and Fresh" sign was off. However, the scent of vanilla, sugar, and fried dough still permeated the evening air. Opening the truck door, I sucked in a mouthful and felt re-energized. Nash joined me on the sidewalk. He didn't pay attention to the donut air, but he never did.

"Giulio must have enemies despite what he says," I said. "I'm going to start with an online search. I'll hit social media, check Reddit, then work my way through more obscure sites."

Nash nodded. "I'll stick with the studio thieves. It's a paying job. You can't lose focus."

"But that's my job."

"I need a hobby, I guess." He shrugged.

"And you'd rather not deal with Giulio."

"I'd rather not deal with Giulio." He stepped closer and took my hand. "But if you need help, just holler."

I nodded, and he kissed the top of my head. As he gazed down at me, I looked up. His eyes darkened. I licked my lips. Rose on my toes. We angled our faces toward each other. But before our lips could meet, I rocked back on my heels. He stepped away. We were on a public street in downtown Black Pine where everyone noticed everything. If we got caught necking in front of the Dixie Kreme Donut Shop, word would get back to Daddy, and I would never hear the end of it. Daddy didn't care how old I was. His house, his rules.

Plus, I suspected Daddy was making up for lost time. Vicki had taken me to California when I was just a baby. I only came home for holidays. By the time I'd starred in *Kung Fu Kate* and gotten the lead in *Julia Pinkerton, Teen Detective*, my hiatus breaks had gone from months to weeks to long weekends.

"I'll be here," said Nash gruffly, cocking his head toward the Dixie Kreme Building.

"I know where to find you." I gave him my *Cosmo* smile, thought better of it, and switched to *Good Housekeeping*. The bloom was not off our relationship rose. We'd gone through a thorny patch recently. I suppose we were waiting for the inevitable fade, but it hadn't happened yet. If I followed Nash up to the office, we'd get distracted.

I had to attend Giulio's garden. It was full of weeds.

FIVE
#PROJECTRUNAWAY

AFTER SAYING GOODBYE TO NASH, I moseyed down Black Pine Street, turned the corner, and tramped down Palmetto where the new-made-to-look-old Albright Security Solutions lived.

Not named for me. Vicki had bought it from Nash's ex-wife. Long story, but in a nutshell, I worked for my mother. Again. Except I was near the bottom of that totem pole. Vicki's gatekeeper, professional private investigator Annie Cox, had carved her eagle eye above me. In Georgia, it took two years of private investigator apprenticeship before losing the amateur badge and graduating with a professional license.

I've also heard there's a test, but I'll cross that bridge when I get to it.

In any case, a judge needed my W-2 and Annie wrote the checks. And now my BFFs also worked at Albright Security Solutions (A.S.S., we discovered belatedly). Tiffany and Rhonda were former hair stylists and nail estheticians, but A.S.S. was a temporary gig for them.

One I feared they enjoyed a little too much. My ginger tresses suffered from a lack of Olaplex therapy. And let's not talk about my nails.

I swung through Albright Security Solution's door, causing the bell to jangle. At the reception desk, Rhonda was shoving her phone and makeup into a (faux) Dior Vibe purse. Her head jerked up, causing her beaded braids to swing and clatter. Her round cheeks grew rounder with her smile.

"Girl," said Rhonda. "I wish I had your job, showing up at quitting time. Or Annie's, for that matter, going on vacation. Where've you been?"

"Hopefully, doing surveillance." Tiffany popped her head out of the back office and strolled to the reception area. She had pushed her blunt, blue-dyed tips behind her ears—better to show off dark frames. There was an extra pop in her step, extra gold around her neck, and extra inches to her height due to the lug sole heels of her combat boots.

"I didn't know you wore glasses," I said.

"I don't," said Tiffany.

"New look," said Rhonda, pulling off her jacket. She moved around the desk. "I got one, too."

"It's...wow. What can I say?" I blinked. Took in the Fulani braids and exposed flesh. "Rihanna?"

"Ya-as," said Rhonda, dancing in a circle. "My girl."

Rhonda had squeezed her generous curves into a tight neon green bodysuit. Someone (I assumed Rhonda) had cut out the sleeves and a circular chunk on one side. The side cutout revealed the bottom of a sports bra (thankfully) and more flesh than was appropriate for Black Pine.

L.A., New York — nobody would look twice. But this was Georgia. I didn't even think it would pass in Atlanta.

"Don't dance like that in public," said Tiffany.

Rhonda stopped dancing. "Rihanna dances in her body suits. Why can't I?"

I decided a change in subject was needed. "I've just come from Giulio's chalet—"

"Why didn't you invite us?" interrupted Rhonda. "I love me some Giulio. The man is hot. He knows he's hot, which is annoying, but that's what happens when you're that hot."

"Why are y'all calling it a chalet?" said Tiffany. "This is Black Pine, not Switzerland."

"It's chalet-style?" I began, then stopped. It was easy to get sidetracked by Rhonda and Tiffany. "The house doesn't matter, except that the police found a very expensive jewelry box in his safe."

"Hang on," said Rhonda. "Why do the police care if Giulio keeps a jewelry box in his safe?"

"How expensive?" said Tiffany.

"It's vintage, gold, and very, very expensive. Once owned by Marilyn Monroe." I blew out a long breath. "It's Vicki's."

"Oh, snap," said Rhonda. "Giulio stole Vicki's jewelry box?"

"I believe Giulio's been framed."

"Back up," said Tiffany. "We're missing some key information. Nash was with you?"

"Yeah...um, he was with me when I got the call from Giulio, so he came with me."

"He doesn't trust you with Giulio," said Rhonda. "I get that."

"He trusts me." That much was true. Nash didn't trust Giulio. But I didn't want to get into that, which might circle back to me and Nash together during working hours. We just enjoyed working together, even though we no longer worked together. Officially, anyway. "Giulio's in a lot of trouble. I thought Nash could help."

Tiffany snorted. "I'm trying to picture Nash wanting to help Giulio."

"Okay, forget Nash," said Rhonda. "I want to know about Giulio stealing this jewelry box."

I explained the optics of the script, the safe, and the Marilyn box. "I need more details from Ian, though. I also want to talk to the detective from Montecito."

"You lost me again," said Tiffany.

"The case started in Montecito. Recently, Vicki's been living there while Kevin works in LA. Detective Carter is handling it. Except right now she's skiing in Patagonia, so I can't get in touch easily."

Tiffany firmed her lips and shook her head while Rhonda grew starry-eyed.

"Oh, this is exciting," said Rhonda. "It's like *Lifestyles of the Rich and Famous* meets *COPS*."

"Not so exciting for Giulio, if he's going to jail," said Tiffany.

"That is the problem I'm going to solve." I moved around Rhonda's shiny green bodysuit to sit at the desk. "I'm going to search for Giulio's enemies. I guess it's someone related to *The Red Circle*. A lot of people would have worked on that film, not just the actors."

Five minutes into a Reddit page, I learned Giulio had a lot of haters. Not really Giulio's fault. That was the price of fame. The internet attracts haters more than fans. However, social media wasn't going to diminish my list, only expand it.

"Okay, new plan. I need to narrow my focus. I'm going to call Giulio's agent."

"Giulio had a party recently," said Rhonda, thumbing her phone. "He's in a lot of Instagram selfies."

"Anyone looking shifty like they'd want to set Giulio up?" said Tiffany.

Rhonda looked up. "That's not a look you'd use in a selfie. Besides, all selfies are a little shifty. The vanity makes you feel guilty."

"You do selfies all the time. You just did a Rihanna post."

"And what's your point?" snapped Rhonda.

"Are they Giulio's selfies?" I asked, trying to get them back on track.

"He had a few, but they're mostly from other people's accounts. I found them by using Giulio's house as a location. He named it 'Giulio's Chalet,' making it super easy for me."

I did a mental facepalm.

"What room was his safe in?" said Rhonda.

"Bedroom closet."

"Some of these pictures were snapped in what looks like his bedroom." Rhonda handed me the phone.

"I can tell by the wall of Giulio photos—that's his master bedroom," I said. "Anyone at the party had easy access to that safe."

I called Giulio. "You had a party."

"Hello to you, too, darling. Have you found who has done this to me?"

"I just started the investigation. Let's talk about the party."

"I have many parties, what is your point?"

"The point is many people have access to your bedroom."

"Darling, I am no monk. But you knew this when you met me. What can I say? I succumb to temptation easily. I promise, when we were engaged, I knew no other woman. Except for the one time—"

"Just stop. When was your last party?"

"Last weekend."

"Why didn't you mention this to us?"

"I didn't think it was relevant."

"Not relevant?" I counted to ten. Giulio was his own worst enemy, not mine. But he made it hard to help him. "It's very relevant. Just like not using your security system is relevant. You make it too easy for people to get into your house."

"I've always been like this, Maizie. *Mi casa es su casa,* you know? I want people to feel welcome. The open-door policy."

More like an open bedroom door policy.

"But I haven't had anyone over since my arrest," he continued. "Don't worry. I am on my best behavior."

"Your arrest was just—" Wait. Better to have him on

his best behavior now, anyway. "I need a list of guests from the party. One of them might have planted the Marilyn box in your safe."

"I see." His demeanor changed. For some reason, he preferred the role of the silly dilettante. But I knew he was more than that. Like most actors, much of his posturing was to conceal his insecurities.

"You must have guessed this."

"I do not want to think badly of my friends."

"Is there a particular friend?" Movement caught my eye. I refocused on the room. Rhonda was bouncing on her toes. Tiffany was shielding her eyes from the gaping hole in Rhonda's bodysuit. She handed me her phone and pointed to a woman photobombing a Giulio selfie.

I gasped.

Rhonda pursed her lips, crossed her arms, and nodded knowingly.

"Heather is in town?" I gasped into the phone. "And you didn't tell me this?"

"Don't be jealous."

"I'm not jealous." I wasn't. In my previous life, I'd been jealous. This was the woman who'd sabotaged our relationship. Giulio's "one time" was actually a long weekend that turned into a month. Or two. Then Heather Holliday had revealed our relationship had been staged for *All Is Albright*. She'd clinched our breakup and my decision to leave the show. She'd also messed with our ratings.

I should thank her.

"Darling, I can't help it if Heather keeps showing up in my life. She's the crazy ex-girlfriend. What can I say?"

"You could stop sleeping with her, for one. Every time you do, you let her back into your life. Plus, it's wrong. Morally and ethically."

"It's wrong of her to seduce me," whined Giulio. "Heather knows how to press my buttons. The good ones, anyway."

"Why am I helping you?" I shouted. "It's like you want to go to prison."

"I don't, I don't. Please, Maizie. I'm sorry."

"This is getting good," whispered Rhonda.

"I have no idea what's going on," said Tiffany.

"Giulio," I sharpened my voice. "If you don't take this seriously, I can't help you. Make a list. Two lists. Anyone you suspect, even if you don't want to suspect them. And anyone who has been to your house in the last two weeks. Maybe more. At least since the last time you looked in that safe."

"Maizie, I never look in that safe. How can I possibly—"

"You're the one who might be going to prison. That should be enough motivation to do the 'possibly.'"

SIX
#SOAPEDOFF

"I'VE NEVER SEEN you like that," said Tiffany. "Impressive."

I rubbed my chest. "Not impressive. I just gave myself heartburn. If Heather Holliday's still in town, we need to track her down. The woman's crafty. I wouldn't put anything past her."

"I thought that was just the character she played on *The Great and The Glamorous*," said Rhonda.

"I think Heather pulls a lot of her character motivation from real life."

"My grandma watches that show," said Tiffany. "Who are you talking about?"

"Heather plays Nicola, the neurosurgeon."

"I thought Nicola was a spy," said Tiffany.

"Just when the government needs her. Sometimes she's also a swimsuit model."

"Makes perfect sense," said Rhonda.

"Heather met Giulio on the *G&G* set. He played the Italian doctor, Giancarlo. When they killed his character off temporarily, he auditioned to be my next boyfriend for *All Is Albright*."

"I thought that's a reality show," said Tiffany.

"I didn't know Vicki was auditioning my love life." A nerve next to my eye spasmed. I slapped a hand over it. "My twitch is coming back."

"Come on, girl." Rhonda patted my hand. "You're over this now. You did the therapy. You forgave Vicki and Giulio. Now you've got Nash, although we find that choice questionable, too."

"Yeah, stop focusing on the past," said Tiffany. "You've got enough going right now to drive you bonkers."

"Hey," I said, feeling a bigger spasm.

"That was pretty intuitive, Tiff," said Rhonda.

"I thought so."

"Your concern is noted." I held my eye and stood up. "I've got to talk to the police. And Heather Holliday."

"Don't be mad, Maizie," said Tiffany. "We're looking out for you."

"Got it."

"Keeping it real."

"Right."

"And another thing…" said Rhonda.

At the door, I stopped but could not turn around. "Yes?"

"Before you meet Heather Holliday, you might want to rethink your current style."

"What?" I whirled around.

Rhonda smoothed her electric green bodysuit. "Heather Holliday is a fashionista. I see her on IG all the time. And she wrecked your engagement to Giulio. You need a power suit, you hear what I'm saying?"

She had a point. Not that I cared what Heather Holliday thought of my new wardrobe. But she needed to take me seriously. Sometimes the clothes spoke for you.

And I was still shallow like that.

"Okay. Good point."

"If you need fashion advice, just holler." She swung her hand to her hip, not realizing the cutout had shifted and centered on her belly button.

· · ·

A LOT of people had access to Giulio's house Framing Giulio with *The Red Circle* script pointed toward a personal vendetta. Heather ranked at the top of my list of suspects.

No other suspects made it easy. And maybe a little too much fun. I'd love to bust Heather. She'd made my life miserable. I was also tired of seeing her romping around in a bikini in those commercials for G&G.

But first, I wanted to talk to Ian again. I hoped he'd introduce me to the Montecito detective. I needed a better understanding of the case against Giulio.

I'd been to Black Pine Police Station many times in the past. Black Pine police knew me from my old TV career and as the child of well-respected (Daddy) and slightly notorious (Vicki) members of the community. They also knew me from cases I'd worked with Nash and from cases I now worked with Annie. Because of those cases, I was not a favorite at Black Pine PD. But I was also not a perp, so they tolerated me as a nuisance.

Except for Detective Ian Mowry, who treated me as a friend.

After checking in at reception, Ian found me and brought me back to his cubicle. With his dark wavy hair, lean build, and milk chocolate brown eyes, Ian's looks reminded me of a young Rock Hudson. In personality, Ian was more Jimmy Stewart. His cubby walls were covered with drawings by his daughter and littered with sticky notes.

"There's a lot of evidence against Giulio." Ian rolled a chair over from a neighboring cubicle. We sat. He tapped a file on his desk. "This is what the Montecito detective, Carter, emailed me. All laid out. My team went with him to Giulio's and found the jewelry box in that safe."

"That didn't seem obvious to you?"

"Most crooks do obvious things like that." Ian shrugged. "I'm police. I like open and shut. Someone is robbed. Victim gives us a suspect. Usually, they're right.

This wasn't a smash-and-grab, it was a domestic. In domestics, the victim knows the perp."

"Except Giulio's not the perp. He didn't even know about the Marilyn box."

"So he says." Ian leaned back and drummed his fingers on the armrest.

"Ian, you know Giulio. He's ridiculous, but he's not a thief. Giulio told me about the joy ride. That's a thing Italian kids do with Maseratis."

Ian's right eyebrow rose. "So in Italy, grand theft auto is just a thing kids do. All kids. Whenever they see a Maserati? Funny how the Italian police saw it differently with his juvenile arrest."

"Shouldn't that be sealed?"

"I don't know Italian laws."

"But Giulio wasn't convicted. Come on, Ian. Couldn't you delay the investigation a bit, just until I can talk to Vicki? I'm sure it's a misunderstanding."

Ian gave me a long look, then leaned forward, resting his forearms on his thighs. "Here's the thing, I don't have a problem with obvious. But it does feel like a setup."

"Totally," I exclaimed. "I knew you'd see through this."

"I see through something."

"What do you mean?"

"I don't want you to take this the wrong way." Ian placed his hands over mine and squeezed. "This relationship between Vicki and Giulio makes the domestic situation tricky."

"Tricky how?" I studied Ian's face. "Wait. What? You think Vicki set Giulio up?"

"Honey, I'm not saying that. It's just…an idea. Worth exploring. I am convinced this is a domestic. And domestics are…messy."

I pulled my hands free from Ian's and pushed them through my hair. "Okay, let me get a handle on this. You think Vicki wanted Giulio arrested?"

"I arrested Giulio based on the evidence I received. It's just…something's off. And your mother…"

I knew my mother. She was a schemer. But I thought she was in a better place now. And what would be the point of having Giulio arrested? "What's her motive?"

"You tell me." Ian leaned back. "Here's what bothers me. According to Montecito PD, Vicki reported the box stolen from her home after Giulio's visit. Nothing else was stolen from the home. That box was pricey, but she had a lot of expensive pieces. It raised some eyebrows with the cops."

"Okay, but that doesn't show Vicki to be anything but the victim."

"Vicki's story changed after her initial charge. She told Montecito that maybe she was wrong about bringing it to California and the piece was stolen here in Georgia. The assistant claimed she couldn't remember packing the box. Evidently, Vicki had left for California in a hurry, so the assistant also couldn't remember not packing it. The staff in Black Pine said Giulio had been over recently, claiming he left something."

Giulio had not mentioned to me that he'd been in both of Vicki's homes recently. But I wasn't going to announce that worry to Ian. "Still."

"Then Vicki flies off to Patagonia." Ian made a zooming motion with his hand. "Where she goes off the grid, leaving Giulio to dangle on the hook."

Shiztastic. "I still don't see how that shows Vicki framing Giulio."

"I'm not saying I think she did." Ian shrugged. "I'm saying if Giulio didn't do it, who else would or could've set him up like that? Maizie, hon', I know this is uncomfortable for you. But they had that sham engagement. A publicity stunt or whatever it was. Can you see them having some kind of dispute where either Giulio steals the box to get back at your mom and your mom sets Giulio up to get back at him?"

"I don't know." I bit my lip. "That seems extreme for either one."

Ian rocked forward again to lock eyes with me. "Do you know how many calls we get where the victim has set up the suspect? Usually, they claim abuse, but sometimes they will claim their lover-spouse-whatever has stolen something. They want them punished for some other wrongdoing — maybe an actual crime or maybe just an emotional injustice — so they invent the crime and plant the evidence to get them arrested."

I opened my mouth and shut it. Took a minute to think. "Is the Montecito detective investigating Vicki too?"

Ian gave me his impassive cop face. "You'll have to ask Detective Carter. He's here. Montecito PD must have a bigger budget than we do. He wants to tie up loose ends. Namely knowing exactly from which home the box was stolen."

"He thinks Giulio did it," I said. "Detective Carter doesn't suspect Vicki. Just you do. Because you know Vicki."

Ian's eyes didn't flicker, and his face gave nothing away. "Detective Carter wants to know which state should convict Giulio. Those are the loose ends."

SEVEN

#HOTDIGGITY

I LEFT the police station feeling a little queasy. The more I learned, the guiltier Giulio appeared. Now Vicki looked bad, too. Asking Giulio why he didn't tell me about his visits to Vicki would prove futile at this point. He visited Vicki all the time. She was still his manager, as far as I knew.

While the girls worked on Heather Holliday's whereabouts, I returned to Nash Security Solutions. The Dixie Kreme Donut Shop was closed, but I stood on the sidewalk before the building and sucked in the delicious bouquet of fried trans-fats. After that hit. I headed to the old door to the left of the shop. Inside, I found a bag of what would be tomorrow's day-olds.

I took them, knowing the shop owner, Lamar, had left them for me. When it came to my donut addiction, Lamar was an enabler. Lamar was also a retired cop who didn't believe in donut addictions.

I'd already dipped into the day-olds as I trotted up the wooden staircase (skipping the sixth stair that sounded like a gunshot). The landing above had two doors. One to a bathroom. The other door had old-timey wavy glass. Nash Security Solutions used to be printed on it until Vicki forced Nash to scrape it off under threat of a lawsuit.

We won't get into that.

I didn't knock before entering like I used to. If I caught Nash half-dressed now, so much the better for me. He had a body like a Greek god and an adorable Jessica Rabbit tattoo on his left deltoid.

Hubba-hubba.

Unfortunately, Nash was fully dressed and sitting at his desk, staring at his computer. Seeing me, he switched off the computer and stood up. "I'm ready for the storage place surveillance. We can grab dogs at Olde Tyme on the way."

I clutched my bag of day-olds and grinned. Olde Tyme Dawgs was a one-room, squat, windowless hovel made of cinderblock, covered in ivy, and located on the edge of the old downtown. As unappealing as the building was, the food inside was killer, and the service was second-to-none. I'd never had a hot dog as a child. I had missed out on a lot. As long as the hipsters didn't get a hold of Olde Tyme and tried to gentrify it, the building would last to the ends of the earth.

"The Braves are playing tonight, too."

My smile faltered.

"We don't have to listen to the Braves. We can do one of your audiobook deals," Nash said, moving toward me. A bare hint of a smile played on his lips and one Paul Newman-blue eye winked. "Or we can just enjoy each other's company."

However much I wanted to hubba-hubba, I had to Giulio-Giulio. "I'm going to do surveillance, but on Giulio. Want to come with me?"

"Is Giulio paying for this case? I'm pretty sure the studio is paying to look for the guy robbing them."

"That's not the point." Even when it wasn't his account, Nash was still a stickler. "Giulio is a friend and there's something very fishy going on. I need to figure it out before either he or Vicki lands in prison."

Nash sighed. "Okay, fine. Let's go."

"Great. We can swing by Olde Tyme on the way to Giulio's. And listen to an audiobook."

. . .

NASH PARKED his Silverado pickup down the street from Giulio's chalet, angling next to a driveway at a vacation rental cabin. With the help of a pair of Bushnell binoculars, we could easily see into Giulio's lighted living area. He paced the room in a pair of black Calvin Klein's and a single earbud, talking and gesturing.

"Who talks on the phone in their underwear?"

Nash shrugged. "It's comfortable."

"I've never seen you talk on the phone in your underwear."

"I try not to talk on the phone except to clients. You don't want to talk to clients in your underwear."

He passed me a dog from the Olde Tyme bag. We chewed in companionable silence for a few minutes.

"Why follow Giulio?" said Nash, turning toward me. "What do you think you're going to learn?"

"He's not telling me everything. That's not unusual for Giulio, but..."

"It feels hinky."

I shifted in my seat to face Nash. "The whole thing is hinky. The Montecito detective's here in Black Pine. I'm pretty sure Giulio is telling the truth, just not the whole truth. But I also don't think Vicki could be trying to frame him like Ian thinks."

"Did you learn any more about the X-factor? Is someone else framing Giulio?"

"His crazy ex-girlfriend was at a party at his house recently. She works on a soap opera that films in California. For some reason, she's in Black Pine."

"Could she have stolen the jewelry box from Vicki's?"

I grimaced. "That I don't know. Unless she got someone to steal it for her."

"Like paid off one of Vicki's staff?"

"Oh right," I said excitedly. "I could totally see her doing that. I was trying to picture Heather breaking into

Vicki's house. She'd obviously wear a full black body-suit, stiletto boots, and a mask. Like Catwoman with all the grappling hooks and whatnot. I just couldn't see her getting through Vicki's security system. I don't think she's that smart."

While we were talking, Giulio had strolled out of his living room. To get dressed, I hoped. His garage door opened, and a Lamborghini drove out. I placed my hand on Nash's arm and pointed. He swiveled in his seat, cranked the truck's engine, and waited for Giulio to drive past. Giulio's Aventador sped down the mountain road. We followed at a more leisurely pace. It wouldn't be hard to spot Giulio's bright red, low-profile sports car among the SUVs, minivans, and trucks of Black Pine.

"At least he's not headed to Vicki's to steal more priceless objects," I said cheerfully. "He would be headed up the mountain, not down."

"Where do you think he's going?"

"He likes to eat at The Cove, like everyone else."

Nash checked his rearview. "Look out the back. I think we've got a tail."

"Why would someone follow us?" I turned in my seat. "I don't see anybody."

"That's why I think they're tailing us. Gray Hyundai."

I spotted the sedan rounding the next turn as we slowed for a stop sign. "There it is. Could be a coincidence."

Nash nodded. "Just keep an eye on it."

"Is there a reason you'd be followed?" I squinted, but the sedan was too far away to get a glimpse of the driver.

He glanced at me. "Why do you think they'd be following me?"

"It's your truck."

He scowled. "Just watch them. Giulio's headed downtown."

EIGHT

#PHOTOBOMBED

A FEW BLOCKS from downtown Black Pine, the Lamborghini turned onto Laurel Oak Street, leading into historic Black Pine's iconic neighborhood. The houses were built at the turn of the twentieth century when all the Gilded Age wannabe robber barons — Northern carpetbaggers and Southern empire builders alike — built their summer homes in the up-and-coming resort town of Black Pine. The real robber barons built their monstrous villas on Black Pine Mountain overlooking what would eventually be Black Pine Lake (after the robber barons' grandkids convinced the TVA to flood the valley so they could also yacht, as well as golf and hunt).

There are other neighborhoods in Black Pine with homes built during the same period. Mostly clapboard cottages, shotgun houses, and log cabins. They housed the lumberjacks, copper miners, farmers, and service workers who made up the year-round population. These neighborhoods weren't deemed historic until someone in Atlanta recently found them interesting, so most were neglected and now consisted of mostly rotting frames and weedy parking lots.

Both sides of my family originated in homes on the literal "other side of the tracks" from historic Black Pine.

Not only does Daddy live on his family's land, but his home is still a cabin. He just increased the land and the size of the cabin by about 100 percent. On the other hand, Vicki chose to "move on up" from her shotgun shack origins to buying the Peanut Mansion on Black Pine Mountain.

I'm sure there's something symbolic of both dwelling choices that a good therapist would find interesting.

Because I was raised in Beverly Hills, I have more of an outside-looking-in perspective on Black Pine culture. To me, it seemed if you wanted to live in historic Black Pine, you still needed a lot of money. If you wanted to live on the mountain, you needed more money. If you lived somewhere else in Black Pine, you had just enough money. If you didn't have any money, you either moved out of Black Pine or in with someone else.

Like me, living with my father's family.

"Giulio's turning onto Magnolia Circle," said Nash. "I'm going to take the alley and cut over to the other end. We should see where he went when we approach from the other side."

Magnolia Circle ran alongside the lakefront. The Silverado cornered into the alley once used to service Magnolia Circle's stately homes. We bumped along, avoiding trash cans and recycling boxes until we reached the end. He took a left to cross back to Magnolia Circle.

"Someone's having a party," I said. Cars were parked along the street and in the circular drive before a two-story, white-washed brick mini-mansion. "Pretty big party, by the looks of it. Good thing they have a valet."

Nash parallel-parked next to the lake. We watched Giulio's Lamborghini stop in front of the valet. Giulio hopped out, thankfully now wearing more than underwear. Valentino's summer collection by the look of it.

"He didn't tell me he was going to a party," I said.

"How does he expect me to help him if he doesn't tell me anything?"

"I think you need to reframe your expectations when it comes to Giulio." Nash studied the rearview mirror. "The sedan didn't follow us down the alley. We know where Giulio is. You want to take a walk?"

"Along the lake? That sounds nice."

"I guess we could do that." Nash glanced at the sidewalk that ran along the lake. "I'd like more cover, though. On the other side of the street, we could slip between the parked cars, if needed. I'm hoping to spot the sedan."

"Oh, right," I said, trying not to sound disappointed.

"I suppose if we held hands, we could act like a couple taking a sunset stroll, though." He nodded. "Good idea."

That was not exactly the idea I had in mind. I needed to reframe my expectations when it came to Nash, too. When we got out of the truck, I didn't take his hand on the sidewalk.

"What's the matter?" said Nash.

"We don't do PDA when working a case, remember? We can act like a couple without holding hands."

"That was one of the rules when we were working together. I'm just along for the ride." He winked at me and smiled, making a single dimple pop in his cheek. "Besides, this is cover."

I took his hand. Mainly due to the dimple. I was weak. His hand felt good in mine — big, strong, and safe. "We're acting like a couple."

"Yep." He swung our joined hands between us as we strolled down the sidewalk.

"The key word being 'act.'"

He stopped walking and turned toward me. "That's not what I meant."

"But it's what you said."

"What's going on?" He clutched my hand before I

slipped it from his grip. "I'm not good at reading between the lines, Maizie. Spell it out."

What was it about? Not being taken for granted? It was hard to remember as his thumb stroked my palm, his arctic blue eyes gazed down at me, and his dimple remained fresh in my mind. There was also the setting sun. The gentle call of birds and the lake lapping the shoreline. The scent of grilling burgers — always a plus.

A slight breeze stirred my hair. Nash reached to move a wisp threatening my eye and tucked it behind my ear.

"I just feel like we're in a rut," I said lamely.

"Okay," he said. "Maybe the problem is, I don't mind a rut. But I'm older than you."

"What about where we're going?"

"I'm not worried about that either." His hand slid behind my neck. "I'm a live-in-the-moment kind of guy."

I wasn't a live-in-the-moment kind of girl. I tried that when I'd outgrown my *Julia Pinkerton, Teen Detective* cheer skirt and the rest of my child acting wardrobe. I'd struggled with wanting to leave my Hollywood lifestyle but not having the *cojones* to stand up for myself. Living in the moment had ended when I stood before Judge Ellis, who kicked me out of California and sent me back to Georgia. In Black Pine, I once again had career and life goals, like finishing my two-year apprenticeship so I could become a private detective. And like getting married, having a family, and trying small-town American normalcy for a change.

Likely, normalcy would never be in the cards for me. Probably not when my career goal was investigations.

But I stood on my toes to kiss his cheek anyway. As my lips grazed his stubble, he moved his hands to my waist, yanked me against him, and spun us a quarter-turn. "Wow, you're really living in the moment."

"Gray sedan." His deep voice rumbled in my ear. "Parked down the street between an Escalade SUV and a blue Tesla. I spotted a flash of light. It's either a camera lens or binoculars aimed at us."

"On us?" Nash's body blocked my view. I squirmed against him to see around his wide shoulders. "Why are they spying on us?"

"Let's do more happy couple acting and get closer."

I grimaced. I'd still rather do happy couple for real. Why couldn't I just come out and say what I really thought?

He spun me around again, squeezed me, and set me on the sidewalk. Holding hands, we strolled along the lake toward the sedan. Careful to keep our faces turned toward the lake or each other, we watched the sedan peripherally.

"When we get a half-block past the vehicle, we'll double back on the other side," muttered Nash.

"I have an idea," I exclaimed. "I'd love a selfie."

Nash had taken a step, but our joined hands kept him from moving forward. He looked over his shoulder, consternation written on his face. "A what?"

"It's a beautiful night." Dropping his hand, I gestured toward the lake. "Let's do a selfie."

"I don't do selfies. Selfies are a symptom of what's wrong with the world..." He stared at me. "Is this the rut thing again?"

I shook my head and began adjusting my phone. "Come over here, big guy."

"Big guy?"

"Your arms are longer. You take the picture." I handed him the phone and positioned myself with my arms wrapped around his waist, a jaunty cock to my head, and a seductive smile.

The "make your single friends jealous" pose—made famous by the Kardashians.

"The camera lens is—" Nash looked down at me. "I have to hand it to you, Miss Albright. You're a wily one."

"Thank you. Smile."

He looked back at the camera, tapped to adjust the focus, and let the shutter fly. Still holding on to each other, we examined the pictures he'd taken of the gray sedan.

The driver's seat was empty.

NINE
#COUPLECAPABLE

"SHIZZLES," I said. "Where did they go?"

Nash scanned the opposite side of the street. "How could they have snuck out of the car without us noticing? We were both watching. I couldn't even tell if it was a man or a woman."

"What now?"

"Assume they're still watching us." Nash jerked his head toward the other side of the street. "Let's mosey over to that sidewalk and take a peek at the car."

Our peek revealed nothing more than the Hyundai was a rental with Georgia plates.

"Fulton County could mean an Atlanta rental or nothing at all," said Nash.

"I still want to know who Giulio's visiting," I said. "It's a big party. There could be suspects."

"We'll speak to the valet."

"Or we could just go to the party."

"Crash the party?"

"It's a party. I know Giulio. He's there. No biggie."

"Is this how Hollywood parties work? Down here if you show up at a party uninvited, it's party crashing. Most folks think it's rude."

"Do you have a problem with breaking a little social custom to help a friend?"

"Not really." He grimaced. "But if I want to work in this town, I need to be professional. Let me find out whose house this is first."

While he tapped on his phone, I checked my outfit. Rhonda and Tiffany were right about my wardrobe. I'd gone from Who Wore It Best to Lake Hair Don't Care. When you spend your nights sitting in pickups, slurping Icees, and eating Zapp's chips while doing surveillance on cheaters and smugglers, you dressed the part — jeans, t-shirts, and trucker caps. My frayed denim shorts were Alexander Wang and my tee Stella McCartney, but my hat was Nash's second favorite Braves cap.

I took it off, leaned over, and shook out my hair. Reached in my bag for my little can of Beach Babe sea salt spray and gave my waves a good scrunch. Pouted my lips to apply MAC's Ruby Woo gloss. Shoved on a pair of Quay oversized shades.

"I'm ready," I said. "Let's go."

"The house is a Vrbo rental," said Nash, then looked at me. "What did you do? You look...fancier."

"I made myself more party presentable."

"I thought you looked fine." He glared at the houses across the street. "You're a beautiful woman. You don't need the extra stuff."

"The stuff gives me confidence. And party crashing is all about confidence."

"I like you in the Braves hat." He scowled.

I grinned, then remembered we were only acting like a couple. And I wasn't wearing party shoes. Jimmy Choo wedges would've helped. But you couldn't have everything.

FROM THE SIDEWALK, stone steps climbed the terraced front lawn to the circular drive. The left-side wing ended in a double porte cochère used for more parking. Nash and I ambled past the stone steps, waited for the valet to move a waiting car, and hurried toward the porte cochère. We entered a tiled hall, followed it through an archway, and found ourselves at a nexus. To the right was another archway. To the left, a set of stairs led to another arched doorway. Conversation and music floated from both rooms. Before us lay a closed door.

"The lady or the tiger," murmured Nash.

"Let's peek through the door," I said. "There's got to be a patio or lanai. Giulio likes to be seen in twilight. He says it's the best lighting for his complexion."

"The problem with these homes is the position of their patio," grumbled Nash, looking around. "You have to look at the lake from a window or sit in your front yard. Nobody sits in their front yard on this side of town."

I patted his arm. "If they had their backyards on the lake, then we wouldn't have gotten to walk along the sidewalk and do a selfie."

"Right." He grinned down at me. "Always looking on the bright side, Miss Albright."

The closed door led to another hall that split toward noisy rooms smelling of food and, bonus, an outside door. Once again outside, we moved between the raised beds of a kitchen garden, snuck through another arched loggia, and entered a flagstone patio.

Spotting Giulio, I raised my hand to wave, then yanked it down. I backed up a step and bumped into Nash.

"What's wrong?" said Nash.

"Don't you recognize who Giulio is talking to?" I nodded toward the raven-haired beauty. An artful twist held her beautiful dark waves. Her tropical sundress screamed vintage, but I recognized it from Oscar de la Renta's summer line. The sweetheart neckline showed off her slim build. A chunky diamond heart hanging on a thin chain nestled in her decolletage. She loved a good neckline. Her cleavage was as well known as her winky smile. Nobody wore shocking pink lipstick or a plunging top like her.

"That's Heather Holliday."

TEN

#PARTYSMASH

"GIULIO'S CRAZY EX?"

"Also the famous soap star."

"I've never watched soaps."

"You don't watch TV in general," I said dismissively. "Giulio saw me, but I think he's waiting for Heather to leave. He's probably afraid of what Heather will do if she sees me."

"She doesn't look like she's going anywhere." Nash glanced around the patio. "There are a lot of people here."

"If Heather and Giulio are here, I probably know other people. Let's do a lap."

"A what?"

"Just follow me." I moved across the patio, nodding and exchanging pleasantries with various people I'd known in the industry. We wound our way through the loose clusters on the patio and into the house.

A few familiar faces were actors who'd landed in Georgia for a series or feature. Several actors turned directors and producers who'd sought creative independence with the opening of new studios in Georgia. One director and three producers who'd also made the Southern Switch and taken on projects here while maintaining their west coast presence. Georgia not only had less red tape and cheaper expenses, the quality of life felt easier. FOMO disease — Fear Of Missing Out — wasn't quite as acute in Georgia as in California.

Therefore, the overall party had a buoyant mood. Less anxious. Less vicious. People were much more willing to talk. Even to an ex-celebrity turned private investigator. Which took a lot more explaining than I wanted. But to get some, you had to give some. While I did the rounds of "no, I'm not studying for a role" and "yes, I am living my best life," I learned the house was rented by Heather Holliday.

Ugh.

And nobody knew what she was doing in Black Pine except holding parties.

"I'd ask her assistant," said Edgar, a writer who was a friend of a friend of a friend of Heather's. "They're the ones who really know what's going on."

"Who's her assistant?" I asked.

"A dude. Don't know his name." Edgar shrugged. "There's a room full of assistants, though. It's like they run in packs when separated from their host. Assistants give me the willies. Maybe because I don't have one."

"Which room?" asked Nash.

Edgar looked doubtfully at Nash. "Do I know you?"

"No," said Nash. "I don't know anybody. I don't watch TV or go to movies."

"That's cool," said Edgar. "I wish more people were like that. Except I'd be out of a job."

"The assistants will be gossiping near the food," I said. "They can't drink much because they have to cart their bosses home."

I'd spent a lot of time around assistants. One was always assigned to me, and Vicki ran through them by the truckload. Assistants could be bullies. They had to be. Much of their job was wrangling myopic narcissists.

"I should have known this," I muttered. "If Heather was in town, Giulio would be falling over himself to be near her. Even while facing arrest and possible imprisonment for a crime he didn't do."

"She's that good?" said Nash.

"She's worse than the character she plays on TV. The soap rags nicknamed her the Black Widow At least until the Marvel series threatened a lawsuit." We passed through another archway, following the scent of food. "I don't get why she's after Giulio again. Unless this is just a revenge thing, and she is trying to frame him."

"I don't understand most of the motivations in this industry."

I flashed him a look. "Celebrities have the same motivations as anyone else — love, money, power. Their careers are at the mercy of the whims of The Powers That Be and how those people perceive their worth. All that anxiousness can push your values out of whack. Particularly when you're surrounded by a lot of other neurotics."

"While you talk to the assistant, I'm going to speak to the folks in the kitchen. The caterer might be from Atlanta, but the others are local. I recognized some of the waiters. I'll hit up the valet, too. They might have heard why Holliday's here."

"Good idea."

Before I entered the dining room, I stopped. Said a quick confidence-building mantra, took some deep breaths, and pulled my shoulders back to lengthen my spine. I tilted my chin up, pasted on a closed-lips smile, and adjusted my shades.

As I entered, the buzz of conversation quieted. Fashionably but casually dressed, the assistants stood in tight knots around a dining room table littered with small plates of half-eaten, picked-over food. They turned to watch my entrance. Almost simultaneously, the crowd's eyebrows half-rose and lips curled into smug smiles. Someone giggled. I ignored the rush of nervousness that threatened to overpower me.

"Hello," I said. "I'm—"

"We know who you are," said a young woman. "Who sent you?"

"Heather," I said. "Heather needs something."

A deep sigh rose from the corner. A youngish man wearing thick black frames and slim-fit whites tunneled through the small mob.

"What does she need?" His voice had the bored lilt of the overpaid and chronically oppressed.

"Walk with me." I turned and halted. A woman looking Instaworthy with caramel lowlights and a fab red mini-dress leaned against the wall near the door, arms crossed. Looking irritated. Vicki's newest assistant. Irritated was her M.O., but she had to deal with Vicki. "Irene. Why aren't you in Patagonia?"

"Vicki didn't need me."

I'm sure my face showed my confusion.

"Are we walking or what?" said Heather's assistant. "This is Heather's party. Heads will roll if Heather is kept waiting. It better be your head, not mine."

I turned to give him a good glare. He glared back and moved through the doorway. I looked at Irene. "I didn't know you were in town. I need to speak with you."

"You know where I live," she said glibly.

She lived with Vicki. In the Peanut Mansion. And in the Montecito modern Mediterranean. The Malibu beach house. The Upper East Side Manhattan apartment. And wherever else Vicki was domiciling at a given moment. Except Patagonia, it seemed.

"I'll talk to you later," I called over my shoulder and charged after Heather's assistant. Before reaching the sunroom, I caught up and placed a hand on his arm. "Actually, I just wanted to chat with you. What's your name?"

"Eddy." He looked at my hand, then looked at me. I yanked my hand off but gave him my *Cosmo* smile. He gusted a faux sigh. "How much are you offering?"

"Sorry, what?"

"Okay, how much does Irene make? Vicki's schedule has got to be more hectic."

"I'm not here to find Vicki a new assistant. I wouldn't steal Heather's at her own party."

"It's been done before." He studied me behind the thick frames. "Then what do you want?"

"It's about Heather," I said tentatively.

"You know better than to ask me about my employer."

"You know I know better. You know who I am." I swallowed my discomfort. "What's Heather doing in Black Pine? Is she interested in Giulio again?"

"Fascinating." Eddy sniggered. "Obviously, I know about the whole love triangle thing. But I thought you were with Lurch."

"Lurch?" I felt my cheeks flush. "Nash doesn't look like Lurch."

"He's big and lurchy. Would you rather me say the Dwayne Johnson-wannabe ripoff? Okay, fine, I thought you were with the salty Rock."

"Nash isn't salty. He's just the strong silent type—" I shook off the direction of the conversation. "Why is Heather in Georgia? Is she filming? Her contract must have outs."

"Of course Heather Holliday has outs in her contract. She's been a veteran on *G&G* since she played Claire Ustinoff's illegitimate switched-at-birth daughter." Eddy smirked. "We're not filming. We're on vacay."

"In Georgia?"

"Mhm."

"Because Giulio is here..."

"Could be." Eddy tapped his pursed lips. "But I doubt she's interested in rekindling. She's on to new fires."

"I saw her just now with Giulio on the patio. And she was at Giulio's party recently."

"What else is there to do in Georgia? Anyway, there are a lot of people here." Eddy mocked a side-to-side glance. "Watching."

"So?"

"Check the tabloids, same as everyone else. That's you now, right? No longer a someone but an everyone?" He scoffed, shaking his head. "You've been forced to quit, so you recast yourself in the same role. Except without the benefits — like insider information."

I caught my gasp, then snapped my mouth shut.

"Whatever." Eddy turned with a waggle of his fingers. "Ta."

I didn't roll my eyes but drew up my chin and threw back my shoulders, ready to glide back to the "in" crowd. I had to get out of this house before I could allow the pricks of that barb to hurt.

He was right, though. I couldn't stand with my feet in two realms. It was humiliating, even knowing I hadn't wanted my old life when everyone knew I'd been forced out. However, Giulio still needed my help. I'd have to continue with the swagger and act like it didn't bother me.

I returned to the patio, searching for Giulio. And bumped into Heather.

She'd been talking over her shoulder to a friend. Righting herself, she studied me through narrowed eyes. "Maizie Albright," she sneered. "What are you doing here? In my home? At my party? Uninvited."

She'd delivered her lines perfectly, using her *G&G* character, Nicola's, voice. The crowd hushed and looked at me.

Shizzles. More humiliation. But I guessed I should expect that possibility as a party crasher.

ELEVEN

"I'M LOOKING FOR GIULIO," I said lamely.

"I'm having déjà vu," Heather laughed. Around me, the crowd tittered. "Is this where I say, 'Too late, honey. He's been with me all weekend?' Don't you get tired of hearing that line?"

I pressed my lips together and counted to ten. "Can we speak somewhere privately? It's about Giulio."

Heather shook her head. "Sorry to be rude, but I am the hostess and you're not a guest. Make an appointment with Eddy. I'll try to fit you in." She stared at me over the rim of her champagne flute and took a sip.

I lowered my voice. "Did you know Giulio is in trouble?"

"Drama follows Giulio. I hardly pay attention."

She took another sip. My gaze followed the flute, stopping at her decolletage. I blinked. Something niggled at my brain, but I couldn't think of it.

"Sorry to have disturbed your party," I muttered. "I'll find Giulio, then I'll leave."

"Whatever." She took another sip and strode into the house.

I pushed through the knot of people surrounding us and searched for Giulio on the patio. I found him reclining on a lounge chair near the pool, gazing at the darkening sky.

"Why are you going to parties when you're facing this kind of trouble?" I exclaimed. "Do you know how that looks?"

"Hello to you, too, darling. I hope it looks like I'm acting innocent of the charges against me, which I am." He drew himself off the lounge chair to buss my cheeks. "Besides, I have complete faith in you."

I didn't. But I wasn't going to tell him that. "What is Heather Holliday doing in Black Pine?"

"I have no idea." He grimaced sheepishly. "Wherever I go, she finds me."

"What about when you were in California — at Vicki's Montecito house? Did Heather find you there?"

"Really, darling. You're so passive-aggressive lately. What are you accusing me of? Or is it Heather you're accusing? You know I don't do vague."

"Don't you realize how suspicious you look? They could have stolen the Marilyn box in Montecito or Black Pine. You were in both places. Now Heather's in both places."

"Vicki's an investor in a production company that's doing a streaming service feature. I can't go into details because I signed the nondisclosure." He sighed. "A week or so ago, Vicki held a weekend at her home for some of the principal actors who were interested in the script. Heather was there, too. Vicki wanted Heather to read for the part, but Heather wouldn't read."

"So Heather didn't get the part?"

"I can't say. Vicki left for Patagonia, and Heather showed up here. Meanwhile, I am facing this injustice. Can you believe it?"

I believed that Heather could be as vindictive as Vicki. Word on the street said she'd ruined plenty of G&G careers when she thought the actors had double-crossed her. Since she openly stole boyfriends for fun, would it be that much more difficult to steal a jewelry box for spite?

"Do you think Heather would have stolen the box and planted it in your safe?"

"I can't believe she'd do such a thing." Giulio gripped my arms. "But if this is true, she can tell the police it's a mistake."

"I bet Heather meant it as a prank. She probably didn't realize it would go this far."

"Can you prove it?" he said.

Before I could answer him, a shriek cut through the drone of voices and music. Several more screams followed the initial screech. We turned toward the house. The people on the patio crowded toward the open doors, seeking the source of the screams. I ran toward the house and stopped at the edge of the crowd.

"Look everywhere," screamed Heather from inside the crush of people. "Everyone look. Get out of my way. I need air." The crowd parted. Heather pushed through to the patio, clutching her neck.

"What happened?" I said.

"It's gone," she cried. "My necklace. I have to find it. It's from the Elizabeth Taylor Trust. My pavé heart necklace."

I gasped. I'd heard Heather collected vintage celebrity jewelry. All of Elizabeth Taylor's pieces had been auctioned at Christie's. Heather must have spent a crazy amount on it. I'd thought there'd been something familiar about that necklace. Richard Burton had Van Cleef & Arpels make a pavé heart pendant for Elizabeth Taylor after she grew jealous of him and Sophia Loren. One of the less famous pieces from Burton's "kiss-and-make-up" jewelry gifts.

Vicki had given me Taylor's book, *My Love Affair With Jewelry,* as a birthday present when I was eight. Likely, Vicki had hoped the former child star's sparkles might motivate my acting career. I loved the jewelry, but at eight I was (and still am) more motivated by ice cream.

Spinning away, I ran to search the patio where I'd

seen Heather and Giulio. I spotted Giulio standing where I left him, staring at the pool.

"Giulio, Heather lost her necklace somewhere. Help us look."

He stared at me, then suddenly pivoted, and strode toward the far side of the patio.

I ran to catch up with him. "Giulio, did you hear me?"

"Leave me alone, Maizie." Reaching the steps that led to the lawn, he stumbled and put a hand out on the stone wall to catch himself.

"What's wrong? Did you have too much to drink?"

"I am too sober. That's the problem." He looked at me over his shoulder, his expression haggard. "I can't believe what is happening to me. It's like the Bill Murray movie with the over and over again."

"*Groundhog Day*?" I grabbed his arm, pulling him around to face me. "What are you talking about?"

He reached into his pocket, took my hand, and poured a stream of platinum and diamonds into my palm. "Look at what's happened to me."

"Why do you have Heather's necklace?" I stared at the slinky loop of platinum that puddled over the diamond-encrusted heart. Then jerked my head up to stare at him. "Did you find it?"

"Yes, I found it," he hissed. "In my pocket. How is this happening to me?"

TWELVE
#CATONAHOTTINGOOF

I CLAMPED my hands around the diamonds and looked over my shoulder. "What do you mean, you found it in your pocket?"

"Just that," whispered Giulio. "I don't know how it got in my pocket. When you ran to see about the screaming, I reached in to find my lighter and found the necklace instead. Don't look at me that way. This craziness makes me want to smoke."

"I don't care about that. Where were you going?"

"I don't know. I just needed to get away, to think… and maybe to hide this?"

"OMG, Giulio. Hide her Elizabeth Taylor diamond necklace? Could you act more guilty?"

"Elizabeth Taylor? What does she have to do with this?"

"Come on." I gripped his hand and yanked him toward the house. "You're going to give Heather her necklace. I'm sure there's an explanation for it being in your pocket."

The only explanation I could think of was Heather slipping the necklace into Giulio's pocket to make him look foolish. Again. Her stupid pranks had gone too far. It was time to confront her. Party or no party.

The hubbub surrounding Heather had grown. My cheeks felt flushed with anger. My heart walloped within my chest. I was terrible at confrontation. But Heather had ruined a relationship with my then-fiancé (even if it was for the best) and was now about to catastrophically ruin Giulio's life. I couldn't let her get away with this.

I was going to stand up to this woman for once in my life.

Dragging Giulio with me, I pushed through the crowd and spotted Heather's sundress. Her back was to us, but by her hand gestures, I knew she told a story with gusto. Doing the drama once again. Reaching her, I felt Giulio tugging. I kept my hand clamped around his wrist.

I tapped her shoulder. "Heather, we need to speak privately."

Still enjoying the drama, she ignored me.

"Heather," I barked, using Julia Pinkerton's snotty teenage tones. I'd found in these circumstances, it helped to draw on my old character, who had no issues with confrontation. In fact, she relished confrontation. Or at least her writers did. "Heather, Giulio and I need to talk to you. Privately."

She glanced over her shoulder, rolled her eyes, and turned back.

"It's about your necklace, Heather," I bellowed. "We have it."

She spun around. "You have my necklace? Where was it?"

"Finally, we have your attention." I glanced back at Giulio, who was doing his best to jerk free. "Giulio, we can't let Heather do this to you."

"Maizie," pleaded Giulio. "Let's not be hasty."

"Get a grip. Heather can't be that good in bed." I turned back to face Heather. "This has gone far enough. It's disgraceful what you've done to this man."

"What *I've* done to this man?" Heather narrowed her eyes. "Can we drop the melodrama and focus on my incredibly expensive and irreplaceable necklace that *once belonged to Elizabeth Taylor?* Where did you find it?"

Talk about melodrama. I opened my fisted free hand and dumped the necklace unceremoniously into Heather's palm. "To save you the embarrassment, I didn't want to say this publicly," I sharpened my tone. "But keep your hands out of Giulio's pants. We all know he's easily distracted, but hiding the necklace in his pocket, then pretending it's missing? That's a low blow even for you. In the morning, I'll accompany you to Black Pine police so you can tell them about the joke you played on Giulio with *my mother's* jewelry box."

The crowd had hushed. Everyone had heard me. But instead of satisfaction, I felt ripples of unease. Another reason I hated confrontation. My stomach gurgled erratically and my hand gripping Giulio's wrist felt clammy. Luckily, he had stopped tugging. His hand dangled loosely in my grip.

Too loose. I glanced back at him.

Giulio's complexion had gone pasty pale with a slightly greenish tinge. His liquid brown eyes looked glazed. And his thick hair had gone limp. I'd never seen him with limp hair before. "Are you okay?"

He shook his head slowly, then continued jerking it back and forth.

"What are you saying?" Heather shrieked. "That I planted my necklace in Giulio's pocket? And what joke with your mother's jewelry box? Are you crazy? Are you telling me Giulio had my Elizabeth Taylor necklace in his pocket this whole time?"

Giulio's eyes widened. His mouth gaped. His body trembled. I let go of his wrist and turned back to face Heather as two men stepped around her. I felt the blood drain from my heated face and sluice to my toes.

"Ian?" I laughed nervously, trying to cover the hammering of my heart. "What are you doing here? Heather was talking to you that whole time...when I was... who's this?"

"Detective Carter." The man, shorter than Ian, but slender-fit, raked his gaze over me. Like Ian, Carter wore a light jacket and slacks with dark shoes, but a brand of sneakers I didn't recognize.

Ian shook his head slightly. The men continued to move forward. Toward Giulio. Who had grown more green. His trembling had turned to full-on shaking.

"I...I mean...who called the police?" I stammered.

"I did," chirped Eddy from behind Heather. "I mean, why wouldn't I? That necklace is priceless. She wears it all the time, even though I tell her she shouldn't."

"Shut up, Eddy," said Heather. "Neither the time nor the place."

"Heather, this was just a prank, right?" I pleaded. "Tell the detectives it was a joke to get back at Giulio and Vicki for...whatever..."

"I don't know what you're talking about." Heather had also paled. She tightly crossed her slender arms over her chest. The necklace dangled from one hand.

"Ma'am," said Detective Carter. "We're going to need that necklace as evidence."

Heather handed Carter the necklace. Taking a manila envelope from his inner coat pocket, he shook it open, dumped the diamonds and platinum inside, and replaced it in his coat.

"Giulio," said Ian. "You need to come with us."

Giulio reeled, and Ian caught his arm.

"I mean, what is happening here? Like right now?" I floundered. "What is going on? This isn't a joke?"

"Not a joke," said Carter. "Giulio Belloni, you are under arrest for attempted theft."

Instead of proving his innocence, I had just gotten Giulio arrested.

This was what I got for standing up to someone for once in my life.

As Ian handcuffed Giulio's hands behind his back, Giulio spasmed and hurled the contents of his dinner at Carter's feet.

Carter looked at Ian. "I hate it when they do that."

Heather cast me a seething glance, spun away, and strode into the house.

"Giulio," I cried. "I'm sorry. Don't worry. I'll figure this out and get you out of this mess."

Still bent at the waist, Giulio looked at me through his fallen hair. "Maizie, I appreciate it, but I think it's better for me if you don't help."

A hand grasped my shoulder. I glanced behind me. Nash towered above me. His jaw had hardened and brows drawn, but his eyes were full of sympathy. We watched Carter clean Giulio's face, then Ian led him away.

"I really blew it," I whispered.

"Looks that way," said Nash. "Come on, let's get out of here."

THIRTEEN
#BUTTERFIELDFATE

"WHAT HAPPENED WITH THE GRAY SEDAN?" I said. "Did you see who was following us?"

We had left the party, intending to accompany Giulio to the police station. Ian had stopped us. A second arrest within the week meant Giulio couldn't make bail. Ian had advised us to go home, get some sleep, and check back in the morning.

As if. How could I sleep knowing what I'd done to Giulio? Nash drove us to the old Nash Security Solutions office. While I called Giulio's lawyer, Nash disappeared, then reappeared. With coffee and a box of donuts.

Love this guy.

"It was Carter," Nash said. "He must have been following Giulio. We just happened to be between the two."

"Frigalicious," I said. "Carter was just waiting for something to happen. But he's wrong. Someone is still trying to frame Giulio."

Nash pushed the donut box toward me. "What do you want to do?"

"I've left a dozen messages for Vicki and Kevin. Vicki's assistant, Irene, is in Black Pine. She might know some code word or something that would accelerate the process."

"Code word? It's not enough to say it's an emergency?"

I shook my head. "Every day, Vicki gets dozens and dozens of emergency and urgent notifications. Most of them are important, but hardly any warrant genuine emergency status. Particularly during a planned break. That's why her assistant triages the messages. But for some reason, Irene isn't in Patagonia. She's here. It's weird."

"The assistant even triages messages from you?" Nash rolled his eyes. "That's what's weird."

"Remember, Vicki was also my manager, not just my mother. Some habits die hard." I raised a shoulder. "Anyway, I want to talk to Irene tomorrow. She didn't sound happy about being left behind. Something's fishy there."

"Doesn't sound fishy enough for this Irene to frame Giulio."

"No," I drew out the word while considering the idea. "That wouldn't make sense. But then, none of this makes sense, does it?"

THE NEXT MORNING, I stood on Vicki's pea gravel drive before the stone monstrosity known as the Peanut Mansion. Instead of traipsing up to the front door, I waited for the gray sedan to park. The Hyundai had turned up Vicki's topiary-lined drive soon after I did.

While I waited, I practiced a quick breathing exercise to calm my nerves. Then visualized the upcoming scene — Maizie Albright presents herself as Vicki Albright's daughter.

Which I was. But my real self usually portrayed this character differently.

Before getting out of the car, Carter took a moment

to study me through the windshield. I folded my arms and stared back.

"Good morning Miss Albright," he said, getting out of the car.

"Detective Carter," I said crisply. "Are you following me?"

"I'm here to speak to Miss Dunn." His features remained impassive. Unruffled. Cool.

I could do the cucumber act, as well. "I'm also here to speak to Irene." I unfolded my arms, refolded them, then forced my arms to relax at my sides. "I hope you've turned this investigation toward seeking the person trying to imprison Giulio. Obviously, they will stop at nothing. Even stealing a necklace and slipping it into his pocket."

"My investigation began and ends with finding the perpetrator who stole your mother's jewelry box. I'm not in the business of proving anyone's innocence. Only finding a guilty party."

"It doesn't strike you as odd that Giulio has already been arrested for burglary, he'd try to steal another piece while out on bail? What's his motivation? He has plenty of money. A reputation to uphold. He has no history of stealing or fencing stolen goods."

"His history includes Grand Theft Auto. That was good enough for the Montecito judge who agreed to a search warrant in Georgia." Carter shoved his hands in his pockets and rocked back on his heels. "I'm sorry that Belloni's gotten you involved. I know he's your friend. It's hard to face ugly truths sometimes."

"This isn't the truth," I tried (unsuccessfully) to keep my voice level. "It's all a big lie. When I discover the truth, you're going to look silly traveling all the way to Georgia for nothing."

"If it's nothing, what happened last night? What if Belloni's hidden a stash of stolen objects somewhere other than in his safe? As we speak, Detective Mowry is checking his records for similar burglaries in your town.

This could get ugly, Miss Albright. Be careful of the toes you could be stepping on."

"You take care, too, Detective *Carver*. You don't know who you're dealing with." The words popped out of my mouth. I felt my pale skin redden. The line came from a *Julia Pinkerton, Teen Detective* scene, somewhere in the fourth season when Julia went head-to-head with a cop after the arrest of her sister. "I mean, Carter. Sorry. Sir."

A lone eyebrow rose. Carter considered me for a moment, then turned to walk up the steps to the front door.

Frigalicious. Now that I was all confrontational, I had to watch out for Julia Pinkerton creeping in.

Stupid acting muscle memory.

I spent an uncomfortable thirty seconds standing next to Carter and trying to visualize myself back into Maizie Albright (Vicki's daughter's version) until Vicki's door swung open. Irene peered out. Still looking Instaworthy in a gym ensemble and phone clutched in one palm. But without the typical breezy or saucy smile an Instagrammer would use on social media. She studied us under lowered brows and with pinched lips.

Carter did his police spiel without the badge flash. She hesitated before letting him in the house and instead looked at me. I felt triumphant. The visualization worked. I must have given off Vicki's daughter vibes. I should've practiced in the mirror before arriving, but no matter. Irene had passed me a power play with that hesitant look.

"We arrived at the same time," I said briskly. "I need to talk to you, too, but I can wait. You might as well answer his questions first."

She nodded and opened the door. Carter looked around the foyer with interest. Vicki had renovated the Peanut Mansion somewhat to its former peanut glory days. A lot of oak and marble with peanut plant motifs in the moldings and parquet floor. We followed Irene into the formal living room. I was surprised to see a hodgepodge of magazines and water bottles scattered on the coffee table. More surprised to see the bar trolley looked like it had been in recent use. The crystal decanters had been emptied and various liquor bottles crammed the space between them.

Vicki was many things, but she was not an imbiber. She knew the perils of hidden calories. She also knew the perils of not keeping one's wits about them.

"Is Connie on vacation or something?" Connie was Vicki's latest housekeeper. Or at least the last one I knew.

"Connie's taken some time off while Vicki's skiing." Irene waved us to the armchairs and sat on the sofa facing us. "How can I help you?"

Carter glanced at me, then turned to Irene. "I'm tying up some loose ends. One of which is knowing where the jewelry box was stolen. When I spoke to you on the phone, you were uncertain whether Mrs. Albright—"

"Ms. Albright," Irene and I chorused. We'd been trained well. After divorcing my father, Vicki dug her heels into singular beholden-to-no-one titles.

"Whether *Ms.* Albright," continued Carter, "had taken the box with her to the Montecito house."

"I mean," said Irene, flipping a long caramel lock behind her shoulder. "I thought she did, but then I'm not sure. Like you said, it could have been here. I pack for Vicki. All. The. Time. She's, like, always going somewhere. It's just a blur of suitcases, you know."

"I'd like to see Ms. Albright's inventory of valuables. I'm assuming she has one for insurance. Then I'd like to cross-reference it with the valuables themselves, to make certain nothing else is missing."

"Why are you assuming something else is missing?" I said.

"There was nothing in the box when we found it," said Carter. "I don't have one myself, but jewelry boxes have been known to hold jewelry. Besides that, after last night—"

"Last night," I exploded. "Giulio did not steal that necklace. You're not even examining other possibilities. Last night was ridiculous. Absurd. Ludicrous."

"Ludacris was there?" said Irene. "I didn't see him."

"I understand your emotions, Miss Albright," said Carter. "Last night was very…shocking. For everyone. We should all be glad that Ms. Holliday's necklace was found quickly, though. That's the good news."

"It was planted on Giulio. It was meant to be found quickly." I gulped air and forced myself into a count-down of ten. Indignation worked for my character, but Vicki Albright's daughter wouldn't do uncontrolled anger. Or tears. I pinched the skin by my thumb to shut off my waterworks and got back in character. "I won't stand for this," I squeaked.

"I have a job to do and a plane to catch. I already told you, proving Belloni's innocence is not my respon-sibility." He looked at Irene. "Let's get that insurance list now, so I can get out of your hair."

WE TRAILED Irene up the curving staircase to the gallery that ran along the upper hall. Irene disappeared into Vicki's office. I moved toward the office door but stopped when Carter didn't follow her. He put his hands on the balustrade and gazed out over the foyer.

"You live with your father, I hear," he said. "Not with your mom."

"Yes," I said, still trying to get a check on my real emotions. And not succeeding. "I'm sure you've seen my saga on the magazine covers. Headlined at a lot of supermarket checkout lines."

"Must be hard. That's a big change in address. Going from a place like this." His gaze swept the Old World foyer before stopping on me. "To your dad's house."

"Cabin. My father and his wife have a cabin. It's lovely. Living there's been a wonderful opportunity to spend time with them and my sister." I shifted toward the balustrade. "I don't have my own place because of my probation requirements."

"I know. When I was looking into the theft of your mother's jewelry box, I read about what happened to you." He leaned on one arm, half-turned toward me. "Sounds like you got a raw deal with your mom keeping all the money you made from your TV work."

"It's complicated. There was a required trust, but…" My skin felt hot and prickly. "Anyway, we're working through it. We're in a better place now."

"Still must burn. Then she follows you out here, buys this big old mansion, and dates your ex-fiancé? Must feel like she's breathing down your neck."

"Vicki and Giulio were seeing each other as a publicity thing for my reality show after I quit…that's complicated, too." I swallowed hard and hugged my arms tighter to my chest. "Anyway, it's no biggie. Everything's just great."

"Mm." Carter nodded. "What is it you drive now?"

I cleared my throat. "A dirt bike."

"Giulio's got a nice place, doesn't he? Dramatic views through that big window. Modern, too. What does he call it? Not a cabin."

I cleared my throat again. "Chalet."

"Right. And he's diving a Lamborghini. Not stolen this time." Carter chuckled. "Look's like it's going well for him. That publicity stunt he did with your mom must have worked."

"Not so well, considering he's been arrested." My lips felt stuck to my teeth. I ran my dry tongue over them.

"Didn't I read that Heather Holliday caused the breakup between you and Giulio? I thought you seemed kind of chummy at the party. Helping her find the necklace and all."

"Chummy? No. We're not chummy. But our issues are in the past." Except she still got on my nerves. Of all the people to have been robbed in this scenario. "Giulio's still chummy with her. Which is why it doesn't make sense that he would have stolen her necklace."

"Right. Because you think someone slipped it in his pocket. But I thought he didn't socialize much at the party. Except with Heather." Carter tapped his chin. "And you."

"There were a lot of people at that party. He mingled. So did Heather." I cleared my throat again. "Excuse me, I must have allergies."

"Oh, is that it?" Carter straightened. I turned to find Irene standing behind me.

"Here's the insurance list." She handed the folder to Carter and turned sullen eyes on me. "Now, what did you need?"

What did I need? I'd lost all my Vicki's daughter-energy. I felt off balance. Emotional. A little distraught. Angry. Kind of frightened. Had Detective Carter insinuated that I had a motive for stealing the Marilyn box *and* the Liz Taylor necklace?

Oh, holy hellsbah. I had a bigger motive than Giulio.

FOURTEEN
#PATAPHONIA

"MAIZIE," repeated Irene. "What do you need? Why are you here?"

"It's my mother's home, Irene." Fighting the urge to chew a thumbnail, I snapped at her instead.

"You don't live here." Irene narrowed her eyes. "Vicki didn't say anything about you stopping by whenever you want."

"I can't come to my mother's home when she's not here?"

Carter looked up from the folder. "Can I see some of these items? Does she keep them in a safe?"

"I can't do that," said Irene. "Not without Vicki's permission. I don't have access to the safe, anyway."

"What do you need to see?" I gave Irene a Julia Pinkerton stare-down. Nobody does contemptuous like a teenage cheerleader-detective. "I am quite familiar with Vicki's things, having lived with her *all my life.* Until just recently, of course."

"Pieces small enough to fit in that jewelry box," said Carter. "I'd like to know nothing was in the box when it was stolen. If we could narrow that down, it'd be helpful."

"Vicki packs her own jewelry," said Irene. "She might have taken some skiing."

"I know what she'd wear in Patagonia," I shot back. "I've been there with her."

Shizzles. I needed to grow beyond this Julia Pinkerton snottiness and get back to the role of Vicki's daughter. I moved down the hall toward her bedroom, trying to do my breathing techniques inconspicuously. Reaching Vicki's door, I tore through the sitting room and into the bedroom, heading for the panic room inside one of her walk-in closets.

"Cool as a cucumber. Cucumber. Cucumber," I murmured and pushed out a few quick breaths. "You're Maizie Albright. Maizie. Albright."

"What did you say?" said Irene.

"Nothing." I looked over my shoulder. Irene and Carter had followed me into Vicki's dressing room. I exhaled. I needed to calm down. No need to get emotional just because Giulio had been arrested so easily and now Carter might suspect I was also a thief.

No biggie, right?

The heavy steel door swung open and the interior room brightened. Carter gave me a hard, piercing look and moved inside.

Craptastic.

My heart pounded, and my stomach clenched. Why was I so anxious? I had nothing to hide. Giulio was my friend and Vicki was my mother. Maybe not the best mother in the world, but I'd had years of therapy to deal with that. We were in a good place. Except her current place was Patagonia. And of no help to anyone.

"You're breathing funny," said Irene. "Vicki said you had a fear of closets. I thought she was kidding. Because that's just...whatever."

"I'm fine." I charged inside to prove my point. Just a windowless, airtight room with a bulletproof door. But, silver linings—it did have a high ceiling, a Persian rug, and tasteful wallpaper. Like a bespoke bank vault. Which didn't help me much. "It's called claustrophobia. And super common. But you're right. It's whatever."

Carter looked over from the video monitors he'd been examining. "Command center?"

"Yes." I blew another breath out and flapped the bottom of my t-shirt. "The security system automatically contacts the police when someone enters. I need to input a code now. Otherwise, the door swings shut and locks us inside until the police arrive."

"I've never been in here." Irene sauntered in and flopped on the velvet divan. "Giant safe and TV, I get. But a chandelier and wine fridge? Someone planned to enjoy playing hostage." She snorted and leaned back against the plump pillows lining the wall.

"That's awfully cheeky to say in front of your employer's daughter." I narrowed my eyes. "The bottles are mostly vintage. Collector's items."

"Meaning Vicki doesn't trust the help to not accidentally drink her Château Lafite Rothschilds."

"No," I snapped. "To not accidentally serve it." Although Vicki did worry about the staff drinking the crazy expensive wine. And after witnessing the mess on the bar cart downstairs, maybe Vicki had a point.

"I heard you and your friends drank from Vicki's collection once. The bar tab cost her around 800 grand." Irene smirked. "Maybe it's not the help she's worried about."

"The tabloids got it wrong. It wasn't 800 grand. More like 100." I flapped the front of my shirt. "Besides, that was in high school. And they weren't really my friends."

"They were your friends until you landed in rehab."

"I had an intensive film and TV schedule at the time and my therapist said it was an act of rebellion—"

"Don't you need to enter the code?" said Carter.

"Right." I wiped the sweat from my forehead and turned to the control panel. "Okay, the security code for the safe room is…" My mind went blank.

"Are you okay?" Carter placed a hand on my shoulder, and I flinched. "Claustrophobia is an actual condition. Let's get you out of here. Listen, I can have the Black Pine police check the insurance list when Ms. Albright returns. I've got enough to extradite Belloni to California and hold him until then. It's not a big deal."

"No big deal?" I sucked in air and squeaked out my words. "How is that no big deal? Giulio didn't do anything and you're going to hold him indefinitely? In California? Can you do that?"

"Of course they can do that," chirped Irene. "All it takes is one judge to sign the paperwork."

Spots danced before my eyes. One judge's paperwork kicked me out of California to live with my father in Georgia and forced me to find a new career.

I was on probation. If I were arrested, they'd extradite me back to California. I wouldn't just go to jail. I'd go to prison.

No, I couldn't think about that. Carter couldn't do this to me.

But he'd done it to Giulio.

He could totally do it to me.

FIFTEEN
#THESCREAMANDI

MY LEGS BUCKLED. Carter helped me to the ground and gently pushed my head between my knees.

"Breathe slowly," said Carter. "What's the code for the police? The light on the screen is blinking."

Giulio. Right, think about Giulio. Giulio's life was about to be ruined if I didn't find who stole these items.

What was the code? The date of my first Emmy nomination. I leaned my head against my knees. Shizzles. Why were all the codes based on dates for my awards? Only Vicki remembered stuff like that. But weren't the Emmy nominations announced the same day Daddy told me he was marrying Carol Lynn? I'd been visiting for the summer and had forgotten to tell him about the nomination...

"It's blinking faster," said Irene. "Should we get out? Is the door going to lock us inside?"

"Seven, twelve, twenty-ten," I shouted.

Carter tapped the screen. The blinking stopped.

"Maizie, we don't have to do this now," reiterated Carter. "I think you need some air."

"I'm fine. It's all good." I pushed my back against the wall and leveraged to stand. Easy to do when slippery with sweat. "I'm sure you'll find nothing is missing in the safe."

"If you're okay, we should get started" Carter opened the folder. "That's a big safe. All for jewelry?"

"Some drawers hold paperwork." I tottered over to the safe. Which reminded me of an upright coffin. But I wouldn't think about that. My legs already felt like jelly. My head, like a leaky balloon. "There are shelves for a few bags."

"Bags?"

"A collection of Hermès and a—"

"Vicki owns a Lana Marks' alligator Cleopatra Clutch. She used it on her last red carpet," exclaimed Irene. "Lana wrote Vicki's name in white diamonds on it."

"In that case, putting bags in a safe would make sense," said Carter. "If that purse is missing, it should be easy to trace with her name on it."

"Unless the thief pops off the diamonds," said Irene.

"I was kidding," said Carter. "But you make an interesting point."

The safe also had a keypad. The Golden Globe for Julia Pinkerton was season six. That would have been January. I lifted the hair from my sticky neck. Right, two nights before Remi was born. My first and only sibling. I'd been so excited that I kept checking my phone throughout the ceremony and missed meeting Lady Gaga.

I tapped on the keypad, opened the door, and gazed inside. Necklaces hung on the door. Drawers lined the interior's midsection. Shelves below and above. A lot to go through. I dropped the hank of hair and flapped my t-shirt. "Where do we start?"

"What jewelry or bags would Ms. Albright have taken to Patagonia?"

"Let me think." I leaned my forehead against the cool metal door. "Simple for the slopes. Diamond studs. Missoma London gold chain, I'm sure. Casual chic for fireside. What did she wear last time? Let's see, I made the trip four years ago…"

"Sounds like this is going to take a while," said Irene.

"No rush," said Carter. "Or we could start going through the list and checking off items that are missing. Then cross-reference with what she had in California. Hopefully, what's left is what she took with her."

Irene was right. This was going to take forever. Forever in this windowless room. I pulled out a drawer.

Carter looked over my shoulder. "Rings." He blew out a breath. "Lots and lots of rings. Going to take all day. All right, let's start."

"OMG, Vicki has a Petrus 2016. That's like 60K."

I glanced behind me. Irene had opened the wine fridge. "Get out of there, Irene."

"I'm just looking." She pouted. "I heard Vicki had a Château Ducru Beaucaillou from the 50s that she bought from the Yul Brynner estate. I don't see it."

"The guy from *The King and I*?" said Carter.

"He had an extensive wine collection at his French estate." I flapped the neck of my t-shirt and wiped my forehead. "But not the point. You shouldn't be pawing through Vicki's collection, Irene. She'd have a fit."

"You seem to know a lot about wine," Carter said, studying her.

Irene slammed the fridge door shut. "I try to keep up with the uh...interests of my...employers." She shrugged and skated back to the divan.

"The wine is on this list as well," said Carter. "Maybe we should check that, too."

Wine wouldn't fit in a jewelry box. But I nodded my head anyway.

THANKS TO THE PANIC ROOM, I felt like I had a terrible hangover — headache, dizziness, and nausea. Or maybe from the dozen glazed holes I'd scarfed on the way up the stairs to Nash's office. But who can say?

"I am no closer to understanding the motive behind

framing Giulio than I am to understanding who the perpetrator is," I said, after telling Nash about my day in Vicki's panic room. "Carter wouldn't tell me what else was missing. He's treating me like a guilty party. Irene, too. Unfortunately, we both have motives and access to the goods."

"Except you haven't been to California since you had to move. You can't go to California."

"Yes," I said miserably. "But if Carter learns the jewelry box was stolen in Black Pine, that doesn't help me much."

"Don't worry about that. You're innocent. Tell me more about Irene."

"How can I not worry? Giulio's innocent too, and look where he is." I swung my arms and wiggled my shoulders. "I need yoga or something. The stress is messing with my spine."

Nash moved around me to rub my shoulders. "Does this help?"

I cranked my neck so I could see him. "You're not a shoulder-rubber. Is everything okay with you?"

"Trying something new." His arctic blue eyes smoldered. "I kind of like it."

"I'm holding a lot of leftover tension from the panic room in my neck." I hung my head and blew out a long breath. "I also didn't get the code word from Irene to contact Vicki. I was sucked into that hunt and totally forgot my purpose. When I got back to the cabin, I called Irene, but she wouldn't answer."

"Avoiding you, or do you think she skipped town?"

"I almost hope she skipped town. She'd look more guilty and move the spotlight off Giulio." And me. But that thought made me feel guilty. "Have you thought about changing careers? Your fingers are like magic. Better than our masseuse in LA."

"I take it the shoulder-rubbing isn't going to lead anywhere, is it?"

"Sorry, I'm too focused on the case." I grinned at my shoes. "But keep rubbing."

"It would help to know where the jewelry box and whatever else that might be missing from Vicki's stockpile were stolen."

"Except Giulio, Heather, and Irene have been in both of Vicki's homes. As well as Vicki."

"What's Irene's motive to set up Giulio? If she wanted to steal the items, she could have just stolen them. If it was to frame Giulio, there's got to be something behind it."

"What if it's subterfuge?" I turned to face him. His hands slid off my shoulders. "Plant stuff on Giulio, so she can rob Vicki. They'll think Giulio took everything and while they're trying to figure it out, she could've sold the bigger pieces on the black market."

"The black market? You think Irene knows where to find fences?"

"I'm sure she's learned a lot, working as a PA to people like Vicki. Sometimes collectors will delve into dirty business to get their hands on certain pieces. Irene appeared to be fascinated with celebrities' collections."

Nash nodded. "Who else has Irene worked for?"

"I don't know. I need to do some background research. Although Detective Carter's probably doing the same. I saw him watching Irene when she was looking through Vicki's wine cabinet."

"That's good. Is he investigating anyone else?"

"I don't think so." I sighed. "He says he's not interested in proving Giulio's innocence. Only in determining if the objects were stolen here or in California. I suppose he'll turn the case over to Black Pine if it turns out everything was stolen in Georgia."

"Let's look at this differently. The motives aren't clear and your list of suspects is growing. What about focusing on opportunity? A lot of people have been inside Vicki's homes. Same with Giulio. Getting a necklace off someone's neck is difficult without them noticing. Unless they're distracted."

He held up a slender silver chain dangling an M. "Exhibit A, Miss Albright."

"You stole my necklace when I thought you were just making moves," I squealed.

"I'm a multitasker." His teeth gleamed and the rare dimple appeared near his scar. "I was doing both. Unfortunately for me, I was only successful in one endeavor."

"Keep it up, Mr. Nash, and your luck could change." I waggled my brows, then got serious. "So, I'm looking for someone who gave Heather a back rub at the party?"

"Something like that." Nash raised his brows. "Unless she planted it on Giulio."

"I'm seeing Heather tomorrow. The girls are coming with me."

"Rhonda and Tiffany?" Nash grimaced. "I can't imagine that being productive."

"Probably not. But I promised they could come. I needed a cover. Heather wouldn't meet me."

"Why would Holliday agree to meet Rhonda and Tiffany?"

"Rhonda's interviewing Heather for her blog."

"Isn't Holliday a big star? And Rhonda's... Rhonda?"

"Um." It was my turn to grimace. "Heather kind of thinks Rhonda's blog is another blog? A bigger, more famous blog about jewelry?"

"Won't Holliday figure that out when you get there?"

"Heather loves to talk about her vintage celebrity collection. As long as Rhonda peppers her with softballs and those oozy over-flattering questions Heather likes, it'll be fine." I bit my lip. "And if Tiffany doesn't smart off. Or get ticked off. Tiffany's supposed to distract the assistant, Eddy."

"Sounds like an award-winning plan." He rolled his eyes. "What are you going to be doing?"

"Looking for clues."

"In Holliday's house? While this fake interview is going on?"

I nodded.

"Should I be waiting on your bail call?" Nash smirked. "Maybe Black Pine PD will let you share a jail cell with Giulio. He'd probably like the company."

SIXTEEN
#BLINGBOMB

WHEN I ARRIVED at the A.S.S. office, Rhonda and Tiffany were waiting. I bit my lip and counted to ten before remarking on their ensembles. Rhonda twirled in a streaky tangerine cropped cami, drawstring shorts, and a long, chiffon-ish open jacket. Tiffany wore her usual but had added more eyeliner and thicker-soled combat boots.

"Um, so yeah," I hemmed. "That's a lot of skin for an interview."

"I know. Right?" exclaimed Rhonda. "I saw Beyoncé wearing this outfit on her Instagram. They call it loungewear."

"It's pajamas," said Tiffany. "When you dyed them, you didn't get even coverage. This is why I don't let you color my hair."

"I ran out of Rit. That's not my fault."

"It's fine. It'll be fine," I tried to keep the panic out of my voice. "As long as you can get in the door, just keep smooth-talking Heather and her assistant. Tell them… you're wearing an emerging designer…and she asked you to try a prototype. You're, um…beta modeling her looks for your blog."

Rhonda tapped her lip. "Yeah, I can totally see that."

"Is Heather really stupid?" asked Tiffany.

Rhonda shot her a look. I decided to change the subject. "Giulio made me a list. I have pored over the people at Heather's party and Vicki's party. Other than Heather, Giulio, and Irene, they don't match up. The guests aren't connected to *The Red Circle* movie either. Who else could it be?"

"A really good thief who's familiar with y'all?" said Rhonda.

"Any thief who watches *TMZ* or *Entertainment Tonight* would know about Heather, Giulio, Vicki, and me. Irene is the oddball." I stopped. "But Ian had said the Montecito police had looked into a cat burglar. I don't suppose the burglar travels cross-country."

"Probably not," said Rhonda. "I'd think there was enough stuff to steal in LA to keep him busy."

"It has to be someone."

"Doubt it's a ghost," said Tiffany.

"Everyone knows ghosts only care about their own stuff," said Rhonda. "Unless it's Elizabeth Taylor or Marilyn Monroe, it's got to be Heather, Irene, or Giulio."

"Giulio didn't do it," I said. "That's what we're trying to prove."

"My money is still on Vicki," said Tiffany.

Rhonda rubbed her hands together. "Speaking of jewelry, Maizie, did you bring your goods?"

I nodded and pulled out a large zippered leather case from my backpack. "The *Finest Pieces* blog is super well known. They use freelance writers, but you need to know your stuff. Did you study?"

"I know enough to wing it." Rhonda grabbed the zippered case.

That statement didn't give me a good feeling. "I sold off some of my bigger pieces to pay for my legal fees. A lot of the award-show stuff was rented. None of these pieces are like Heather's Liz Taylor necklace. Just run-of-the-mill jewelry."

"Run-of-the-mill?" Tiffany cocked her head toward

me. "This stuff doesn't look like it comes from Claire's two-for-one bargain bin."

"Everything I have now was a gift. I know when you're short on money, you should sell the jewelry. And I totally did. But it'd be terrible to sell gifts. That would be rude, right?"

Battling feelings of guilt and a weird sense of homesickness, I chewed a thumbnail while they pawed through the jewelry. I missed wearing the pieces, but jewels hadn't seemed appropriate accessories in my new life. They also didn't go with my new wardrobe, which consisted of my most casual designer clothes paired with what I could now afford from Black Pine's Classy Closet.

Although Classy Closet did have some cute duds.

"Can I wear this?" Rhonda slipped a tiara on her head.

"Um, not sure it goes with the loungewear?" I said. "What about the Mateo gold chains? In the last year of *Julia Pinkerton*, the costars exchanged monogram gifts. Aren't they cute?"

"They have diamond M's on them. You've got nothing with R's. What about this?" Rhonda held up a triple strand of Mikimoto pearls.

"I couldn't sell them because they were a gift from Fuji TV when I did *Pop Up!*."

"I didn't ask why you have them," said Rhonda. "But the backstory is good. I might use it."

"I like this," said Tiffany, grabbing a Bea Bongiasca amethyst and chartreuse leather choker.

"That was from a club owner. But those Jennifer Fisher gold hoops are nice, right? Modern yet classic. A director of a TV movie that never aired gave me those."

"Gold hoops? I got my own gold hoops." Rhonda planted a hand on her hip. "Do you want us to wear these or not?"

"Yes." I shook my head. "Wear what you want."

Rhonda grabbed the tiara, pearls, a Bulgari serpent watch, and a Boucheron hedgehog ring. "I'm going to mix styles. Celebrities love that."

I bit my lip.

"I wish you had more leather," said Tiffany. "I'm not really into bling."

"I also brought some books. Beth Bernstein's *If These Jewels Could Talk* is so fun. All about celebrities and their baubles." I pulled out the hardcovers and laid them on the reception desk. "Oh, *Hidden Gems — Jewelry Stories From the Salesroom*, like a jeweler's *Kitchen Confidential*. And of course," I smoothed the cover, "Liz Taylor's *My Love Affair With Jewelry*, which kind of started my obsession."

Rhonda glanced at the books. "Don't think we'll have time for these, Maizie."

"But..." I stared at the books and felt a sad sort of desperation. "You don't even want to look at them?"

"Nope," said Tiffany. "Let's go. I want to get back in time to watch *G&G*. Rhonda got me watching it and now I'm hooked."

I THOUGHT for sure the tiara would be a deal breaker. Smirking Eddy opened the door, but Heather had appeared two steps after him and ushered them in. I waited three minutes, then knocked. I'd been prepared for Eddy, but a woman, Sue, opened the door. Nash had called his old client after seeing her at the party. Sue was doing a stint as a housekeeper and cook. Apparently, Heather Holliday was not Sue's favorite either.

"May I use your bathroom while I wait for my friends?" I announced my alibi, projecting my stage voice.

"Don't move anything," muttered Sue. "Heather makes me measure each object and piece of furniture before I dust and vacuum. She says her third eye can tell if it's been moved a millimeter. It throws off her chi."

My skin prickled. "Can she really tell?"

"Rich people are crazy. But she pays well." She pointed me toward the master suite. "I need to go back to the kitchen. I'm making scones, and Miss Heather wants them the size of her right hand."

"Why?"

Sue shrugged and turned away.

I slipped up the stairs and entered Heather's suite. Shades of blue, cream, and coral — nothing exactly matched but all blended perfectly. Maybe Rhonda had a point with the tiara, pearls, and loungewear. A rug had vacuum tracks creating the letters HH. Her Daytime Emmy had its own stand, which seemed like a lot of extra baggage. But as Sue said, rich people were crazy. I tiptoed around the rug and into the bedroom.

Everything was tasteful, peaceful, and uncluttered. Her dressing room was orderly. A mid-sized safe made me wonder if Heather had traveled with her vintage celebrity jewelry, like her Emmy. I quickly exited the walk-in before it gave me hives. I circled the bedroom and stopped beside her plush bed. A Bluetooth picture frame stood on the nightstand. I watched the carousel of photos and short videos. Most were of Heather. Also, a few family photos and more than a few of Heather and an actor I remembered from another network's soap.

Light from the revolving picture frame glinted off a monogrammed Zippo lighter lying on the nightstand. The etched letters were hard to read as the light bounced off the stainless steel. Afraid to touch it, I squatted to eye level, then blocked the light with my hand to make out the inscription. GIB.

Giulio Ignazio Belloni.

Downstairs, the doorbell chimed. I shot to standing and crept out of the bedroom, around the rug, and toward the open door. Hearing murmurs, I slipped into the hall, rounded a corner, and ran into Irene coming up the back stairway.

"What are you doing here?" I stammered.

Irene's face reddened. "Why are you here?"

"What's that?" said Eddy, bustling up the stairs.

"Who's there?" called Heather.

I felt trapped in an Abbot and Costello comedy.

Irene turned. "Eddy, did you know Maizie is here?"

"Um, where's Tiffany?" I said.

"Who's Tiffany?" said Eddy. "Detective Carter, I think we need some assistance."

"Detective Carter?" All the blood sluiced from my brain to the bottom of my stomach, then dropped to my toes. I put a hand on the wall to steady myself.

"I'm Tiffany." Tiffany stamped up the stairs behind Eddy. "I've told you that like ten times. Sorry Maizie, he and this snooty girl were drinking mimosas by the pool, but when she slipped off, he ran after her."

"Eddy, you've been drinking?" hollered Heather. "It better not be my Armand de Brignac."

"Just Cristal," snapped Eddy. "I'm not allowed to have a friend over?"

"Is that in your contract?" Heather poked her head around Eddy and elbowed Tiffany out of the way. "Maizie, why are you in my stairway? What's going on?"

Rhonda popped up on the step behind Heather. "Miss Holliday, we're not done with the interview. I've never seen Maizie before in my life." She straightened her tiara. "My name is Chardonnay Phillips, and I have a famous blog."

Eddy rolled his eyes. Irene pressed her lips together.

Carter pushed his way past Rhonda. "Do we want to do this in a roomier area and not a stairway? Everyone, into the kitchen." He stood against the wall but blocked my way when I tried to pass. "What were you doing upstairs?"

"Looking for a bathroom. I asked when I came in."

"Just because you asked doesn't make it true."

I swallowed hard and scurried down the stairs.

In the kitchen, Heather looked over a tray of scones.

"Honestly, Sue, how big do you think my hands are? I have slender bones."

Sue gave me a look and stalked out.

Carter revolved his gaze over the group, then leaned back against the wall and crossed his arms.

"Heather, I'm sorry for the duplicity. I'm a private detective," I said. "Apprentice, actually. These women also work at our investigations office, Albright Security Solutions."

"Sounds fake," said Eddy. "If you're an apprentice, why is it in your name?"

"Not my name, Vicki's name. She bought it from Nash's ex-wife, who was...the whys and hows don't matter. The point is, I'm investigating."

"Investigating me?" exclaimed Heather, narrowing her eyes. "You have some nerve, Maizie. I always thought you were soft in the head, but now I'm wondering if you're certifiable. Like criminally insane."

"I am not. I can prove it. I've had loads of therapy."

"See what I mean?" Heather turned to Carter. "She's under a doctor's care."

"Not anymore. Stop being spiteful. I'm looking for anything that will help Giulio's case."

"Giulio stole my necklace." She gasped. "Unless you did it. And you're looking to steal more. OMG. Detective Carter, arrest her."

"I'm not going to arrest her." Carter studied me. "Not yet anyway. Maizie, you and your friends need to leave."

I gasped. "You can't believe I have anything to do with the robberies."

"It seems like he can," said Rhonda, adjusting her tiara. "But if I didn't know you—"

"Rhonda!"

"Everyone keep their mouth shut," said Tiffany. "I don't trust cops. They'll use anything you say against you. We should get out of here."

"See what I mean?" Heather pointed at Tiffany. "Something a criminal would say. Arrest them."

"We're going." I pushed Rhonda and Tiffany toward the door before Carter changed his mind.

Leaving behind a colossal mess. A mess I didn't think I could clean up.

SEVENTEEN
#CLUEDIN

"I DON'T THINK this case could get much worse," I said once we were safely ensconced in Tiffany's car and driving back to the office. "I'm waiting for Carter to arrest me. He'll probably say Giulio and I were in it together to get back at Heather and Vicki or something."

"It's like Heather's taking notes from Nicola on *G&G*," said Rhonda. The pearls were off, but the tiara remained tilted at a rakish angle. "That woman is treacherous. But not as much as her evil twin. And Heather also plays the evil twin, so she's learned a lot about ruining people's lives from that soap."

"I don't trust that Eddy either," said Tiffany.

"He's shifty," agreed Rhonda. "Although if I could get away with it while working, I'd drink mimosas by the pool, too."

"I still think Vicki's got something to do with this," said Tiffany. "She's the only one smart enough to pull this off. Look how convenient it is for her to be gone and completely unavailable while all this goes down."

"Why would Vicki do it? I know she's crazy like a fox and slick as all get out. Sorry, Maizie." Rhonda turned in her seat to pat my shoulder. "But what would Vicki get out of it?"

"Come on, Vicki could have arranged something like that. Irene's hanging at Heather's. She's treating Vicki's house like it's her own," said Tiffany. "How would Vicki feel about Heather chasing after Giulio? You said Heather was at Vicki's house in Montecito recently. Maybe Heather and Giulio did something that ticked Vicki off."

"That is a possibility," I drew out the words while my mind spun. "Giulio said Heather wouldn't read for Vicki's production. But that's not a reason to ruin lives like this. Giulio's arrest is already in the news." My forthcoming headline would make Giulio's humiliation even splashier.

Rhonda thumbed her phone. "Did Giulio tell you that *G&G* wants a wider audience? This article says *G&G*'s producing a streaming series that spotlights different stories. In one of the story arcs, his Giancarlo character reunites with Heather's Nicola. Hulu bought the rights."

"Wait! What?"

Tiffany braked, causing everyone to jerk forward in their seats. "Don't shout while I'm driving."

"No, he didn't tell me," I continued. "At least not the whole story."

Which was par for Giulio's course. But also on me. I hadn't done my due diligence. When it came to Vicki, Heather, and Giulio, I should have checked *Variety* foremost. "Giulio said Vicki's production was also streaming. The one where Heather refused to read."

"Maybe Heather wouldn't read because she already signed for the Hulu show," said Rhonda. "Says here filming hasn't started yet. Maybe Giulio was going to surprise you with the release."

"Vicki paid *G&G* to break Giulio's contract so he could do *All Is Albright*," I explained. "I was the last to know, as usual. But whatever it cost Vicki, she made it back times ten with *All Is Albright*. He was a very popular character as my fiancé. But if Giulio is back on *G&G*, she'll take that as a stab in the back, particularly after Heather refused to read for Vicki's show. That would have been embarrassing for Vicki."

"So maybe Vicki stabbed Giulio right back?" said Tiffany. "By making sure he does some time in the slammer."

"Boy, will Vicki be surprised when she finds out you're going to jail right along with him." Rhonda patted my shoulder again. "Sorry, Maizie."

THE GIRLS HAD DROPPED me off at the old office where I tore through another bag of day olds while waiting for Nash to return.

At this rate, they were going to have to roll me into prison.

I felt frantic. If I couldn't prove that Giulio hadn't done it, how was I going to prove my innocence as well?

The door opened. Nash paused before entering. "You're going to wear out the floorboards. That's my job."

My way of thinking didn't seem to be working. I applied Nash's method—muttering while pacing.

"It's like there are too many motives," I said. "It's a bad version of *Clue*."

"Could be worse," said Nash. "In *Clue*, there's always a Mr. Boddy."

"A shorter prison sentence for me, then. Yippee."

He grabbed my hand and swung me to the couch. "You're not going to prison, and neither is Giulio. You need a fresh look at the evidence — two expensive celebrity-owned pieces were *presumed* stolen and found."

"But we don't know if anything else was stolen or missing."

"My keyword was *presumed* and that centers on all these revenge motives."

"Oh, right? If something else is stolen, they would plant the object on Giulio. He's in jail, so that doesn't work. If anything else was stolen, we'd know the motive isn't revenge." My excitement plummeted. "Unless it's planted on me." My gaze darted around the room. I shot to my feet.

Nash pulled me down. "They planted the jewelry box in Giulio's house. The necklace on his person. Both probably done during a party. I think you're safe. You don't have a house and nobody other than your friends knows you hang out here."

"Except Vicki."

"Who's in Patagonia. She wouldn't do this to you. For practical reasons, if not personal. Have you left her another message?"

"Yes. I didn't get the password from Irene, but I realized I had another way of reaching her — Kevin. I don't know why I didn't think of Kevin before. I'm not used to having a stepfather."

Nash released my hand to put his arm around my shoulder and pulled me into his large, solid frame. "See, things are looking up. Kevin will get Vicki to clear up some of this confusion."

"In the meantime?"

"Fresh thoughts on the case, Miss Albright." He kissed the side of my head. I turned to gaze into his Paul Newman-blue eyes. "Like you said, if the motive isn't revenge, what else could it be?"

"Money. Except nothing's been stolen." I leaned to kiss him, then pulled back. "Or has it?"

EIGHTEEN
#DESPERATEMEASUREMENTS

EITHER SOMEONE WAS LYING, or Suspect X was still out there. Suspect X could be an enemy of Giulio's or Vicki's or just a random thief. However, I had no time to pursue those trails. I hadn't heard from Vicki or Kevin. Detective Carter was flying back to California later that day. According to Ian, Carter was arranging Giulio's extradition and flight plans. He'd also asked Ian for my probation officer's number.

After learning that, even donuts couldn't do their trick.

My suspects needed a push. As did I. Every time I faced them, I completely blew the job. My ego was battered, my stomach was in a vise, and my nerves frayed worse than my Levi 721s. I didn't want to confront the Rat Pack — Heather, Irene, and Eddy — again, but I had to find a way to cut through the prevarication and outright deceit.

I didn't like relying on my old playbook — or should I say, scripts — however, I'd done plenty of denouements on *Julia Pinkerton, Teen Detective*. I could play the part again, as demoralizing as it was to rely on a (fake) teenage cheerleader detective to figure this out. For once, I wanted to solve the case, not myself as someone else.

Which sounds slightly schizophrenic, so never mind.

But I created a plan anyway, using notes from Julia Pinkerton (with a dash of *Columbo*). After explaining my suspicions, I convinced Ian to allow (a cuffed and supervised) Giulio to face those who might have framed him. Ian and Nash had both pointed out (unhelpfully), I could also sink Giulio and his career for good. And possibly land myself in prison as an accomplice. My rap sheet already listed aiding and abetting a previous fiancé.

In other words, my plan could make everything very much worse.

But I was out of ideas. So on with the show.

When Irene opened the door to the Peanut Mansion and gave me a scathing glance, I'd readied to play Vicki's daughter again.

Which I still was. But whatever.

"What are you doing here, Maizie?" said Irene. "I thought you'd be in jail by now. Are you stopping by to leave a note for your mother to bail you out when she returns from Patagonia?"

"Kevin is bringing Vicki home."

"What do you mean?" Irene's voice rose. "I thought she wasn't returning until next week."

Ignoring her hysterics, I swept past Irene with Tiffany and Rhonda on my heels. Nash followed slowly, walking in with Ian and Giulio. "I expect she'll clear up everything when she gets here. If you're worried about the mess, you have a few minutes to clean before the rest arrive."

"The rest?"

"Heather Holliday and I think you're acquainted with her assistant, Eddy? Weren't you day drinking poolside with him yesterday?"

"Oh, snap," said Tiffany.

Bossing around Irene felt sweet, but I couldn't get too salty. Doing "Vicki's daughter" only worked if I could keep the upper hand. With this case, every time I thought I had an advantage, I was trumped.

The doorbell gonged. Nash opened the door. Heather breezed in wearing another Oscar de la Renta sundress. Eddy stalked in behind her. Carter slipped in before the door closed.

"You weren't invited, Detective Carter, but for some reason, I thought you'd show," I said. "You're always two steps behind me."

"Or two steps ahead," said Eddy.

Giulio threw Carter a dark look and muttered in Italian.

"Giulio's looking a little green," said Carter.

"I won't say anything without my lawyer present," said Giulio.

"Good idea," said Nash.

"Or say it in Italian," said Rhonda. "Although we didn't need a translator to understand what you just called Detective Carter."

"Well, where's Vicki?" said Heather. "I don't see why I need to be here. Vicki had nothing to do with Giulio stealing my necklace. If anything, we're both victims."

"Are you though?" I said in my Julia Pinkerton "confess now" voice.

"Yes." Heather arched an eyebrow.

"Anyone could put the necklace in Giulio's pocket. But only someone whom Heather would allow near her neck or an experienced thief could get that necklace off. This could point to Giulio, Eddy, or yourself, Heather."

"As if." Eddy rolled his lip. "I've never touched Heather's neck."

"Like I would allow that," said Heather.

"My point is, who else could it be?" I said irritably. Columbo never had these interruptions.

"The point is, I've been victimized," said Heather. "The necklace was irreplaceable."

"Your necklace was recovered," pointed out Nash.

"It's still in evidence." She stroked her bare neck and gave him a glossy smile. "I feel naked without it."

"Everyone to the living room," I snapped. "Hopefully, Irene's cleaned up after whatever party she's recently thrown."

While they assembled themselves on the furniture, I positioned myself before the marble fireplace. Staging myself so I could clearly see the faces of each cast member.

I mean suspects.

"While we wait for Vicki, let's run through some fun facts. That way, you can correct me if I'm wrong."

"To help Detective Carter's case against me? No, thank you Maizie." Giulio rose. Ian pushed him down.

"Giulio, you've been the most difficult to get the truth from." I placed my hands on my hips. "You didn't tell me about Vicki's streaming deal that was discussed at her Montecito dinner party until it was almost too late."

"What does it have to do with anything?" said Giulio.

"Motive. The motive points toward the real criminal."

"You know we can't talk about those deals," said Heather. "We have contracts with NDAs."

"And you, Heather, refused to read for Vicki at that dinner."

"Why should I read?" She wrinkled her nose. "I don't read anymore."

Eddy shot me a smug look.

I ignored Eddy. "Particularly for the role you've been playing on *G&G*? We read about the Hulu deal in *Variety*. One where the script resurrects Nicola and Giancarlo's love affair?"

"What of it?" She chuckled. "Are you worried we're resurrecting the real love affair?"

"Not really. I happened to see the digital frame by your bed. I saw your pictures of Sebastian Alonzo. You make a cute couple, even though you're from rival soaps."

Giulio gasped. "Alonzo? No."

Eddy and Irene leaned forward in their seats.

"This is better than one of those reunion shows," murmured Rhonda.

"I'd enjoy it more if Andy Cohen hosted instead of Maizie," muttered Tiffany.

"My photo montage is private." Heather's lips thinned. "You were trespassing."

"Your housekeeper let me in." I cast a glance at Carter. "At the party, you made quite a show of spending time with Giulio. Then Eddy said something interesting about you being on to 'new fires' and how there were 'people watching.' I think he meant Alonzo."

"Eddy," cried Heather.

"Were you using me, Heather?" Giulio stood up. "Or messing with me? Who's playing Giancarlo? Me or that *stronzo*, Alonzo?"

Ian pushed him down.

"I wondered the same thing," I said cheerfully. "Maybe she wanted to make Sebastian jealous. There'd be plenty of social media snaps from the party. Or maybe it was a way to get back at Giulio for originally ditching his role as Giancarlo to play Maizie Albright's love interest. Didn't your ratings drop after Giancarlo died?"

"When the writers had to kill off Giancarlo, Nicola's character became a back-burner on *G&G*. That's not Heather's fault," said Eddy. "Nicola had Giancarlo's secret baby two years before. They couldn't do that again. Anyway, the fans wouldn't want her to move on from Giancarlo so quickly."

"Shut up Eddy," said Heather.

"Funny thing," I continued. "I also saw Giulio's lighter on the bedside table next to the pictures of you and Sebastian. Giulio discovered the necklace in his pocket when he'd reached for his lighter."

"Someone found the lighter," exclaimed Heather. "I planned to give it back to Giulio."

"Likely story." Forgetting he was cuffed, Giulio tried to cross his arms and collapsed back against the couch.

"Was that someone, Eddy?" I said. "He and Irene have also been on the scene, so to speak."

"What does that mean?" said Irene.

"The two of you have been chummy. I suppose there's a lot of commiseration, considering your employers."

"Vicki treats you well, Irene?" said Heather. "I'm surprised."

"Right." Eddy rolled his eyes.

"If you're not happy, Eddy, I can find someone else."

"Heather, just to let you know, I'm better at keeping secrets," said Irene smugly.

Eddy whipped his sneer from Heather to Irene. "Are you trying to take my job?"

"I have a feeling you're both going to be looking for employment," I said. "Irene *is* good at keeping secrets. Considering the mess in this house and her caginess about Vicki, I think she must be keeping a pretty big secret."

"Like she's house squatting?" said Tiffany.

"Shh." Rhonda elbowed her. "Remember, we're not allowed to talk during Maizie's monologue."

"Enough," said Carter. "Where is this going?"

"I'm glad you asked." I exhaled, trying to remove the flutters from my stomach. "To know the real motive, we need to know what's missing from Vicki's safe."

"I won't reveal evidence from an active case," said Carter.

"I think we can humor her," said Ian. "I only gave her an hour before I take Giulio back to his cell."

Giulio's Italian mutterings weren't lost on anyone.

"It's okay. Detective Carter doesn't have to say anything." I moved toward the doorway. "I can show you."

NINETEEN
#RATPACKATTACK

THE PANIC ROOM made me more panicky with the number of people crowded inside. My brow beaded with sweat, but not just from claustrophobia. If my plan didn't work, Ian would haul Giulio back with him. I'd probably be hearing from my probation officer soon after.

Nash laid a comforting hand on my shoulder, quieting my nerves. After opening the safe, I pointed toward a small drawer. "This should hold a ruby and diamond cocktail ring from the Duchess of Windsor collection. Last night, I realized I couldn't remember seeing it when we went through the safe."

"No way," screeched Irene. "Vicki has Wallis Simpson jewels? I know Sotheby's sold them after she died, but that was in the eighties. Who did Vicki trick to get a Wallis Simpson ring?"

"I didn't know about this ring," said Carter. "It wasn't listed on Ms. Albright's insurance."

"It wasn't on Vicki's list because it's not Vicki's. It's mine." I continued apologetically, "A gift from Vicki, so I couldn't sell it."

"Maizie, no one cares if you kept your jewelry, despite the fact that you're broker than the tooth fairy in a meth house," said Tiffany.

"I'm glad she held on to the family jewels," said Rhonda, adjusting the tiara she still wore.

"I only kept the gift jewelry," I said to Nash. "It didn't seem right to sell gifts."

He gave me a look that said, "Get on with it."

"Other than me, the last people in this room were Irene and Detective Carter. And behold, the ring is..." With a flourish, I pulled on the handle, pointed, then took a double-take at the velvet-flocked lined drawer. "Right here?"

I felt the crowd tighten around me. Unfortunately, to admire the ring, not to admire my detective work. Quite the opposite, actually.

"Actual royal jewels," said Irene.

"I can't believe you didn't bring the ring for us to wear," said Rhonda.

"I can," said Tiffany. "You still haven't given back the crown."

"I'll make you an offer," said Heather. "You don't deserve a ring like this."

"Another piece for your collection?" I said. "I saw the size of your traveling safe."

"When you were looking for the bathroom?" sniped Heather. "In my closet?"

"The point is," said Carter. "The ring is there. Enough of this nonsense. Giulio needs to return to lockup. I've arranged for transportation for your extradition to California. Black Pine

Police are waiting on the paperwork."

"But..." I stammered. "How do we know nothing's been stolen? Irene, get that list again. We'll all go through the safe one piece at a time."

"That took all day," snapped Irene. "I'm not doing it again. Fine, you caught me. Vicki fired me before she left for Patagonia."

"Congratulations, Maizie," said Heather. "You've revealed nothing important."

I glanced at Nash. He patted my back, then pushed

our way out of the room. We straggled through the dressing room, out of the bedroom, and down into the foyer.

"Maizie, it's been real," said Heather. "Don't ever contact me again or there's a restraining order in your future. Detective Mowry, did you catch that about the restraining order?"

Looking uncomfortable, Ian nodded.

"I know Maizie revealed all that about Sebastian Alonzo, but he's in Mexico, working on a feature. While I'm still in town, would you want to stop by for a drink?" She ran a hand down Ian's lapel. "It's just that since I met you at my party, I've felt so much safer."

Eddy smirked. "Is dating a cop such a great idea? Remember all those rules about evidence in plain view?"

Ian shot me a startled look. But I was too focused on the other cop. "Hang on. Just one more thing. Detective Carter, ever since I met you, you're always turning up wherever I go. At first, we thought you were following Giulio. But after he was arrested, the pattern continued. Have you been following me?"

"Unfortunately, I've had my suspicions about you," said Carter. "You wouldn't be the first child of a celebrity to fall into criminal behavior. You do have a record."

"I was the celebrity," I said hotly. "Vicki was my manager. And mother."

Like sharks, the group collectively tightened around my floundering.

"Miss Albright," muttered Nash. "You're losing focus."

"Where's Vicki, anyway?" sniped Irene. "You said she'd clear everything up."

"Kevin's bringing her back." Unfortunately, I just didn't know when. "Okay, so the ring was still there. But that doesn't mean Giulio's guilty. From the start, I thought there was something fishy. Ian, I told you collectors have been after the Marilyn box for years. They've hired professional burglars in the past. What's a better motive than revenge? Greed."

"Why would a burglar put the box in Giulio's safe?" said Carter. "Why would someone steal Heather's necklace and put it in Giulio's pocket? They can't steal evidence."

"Exactly," I blurted. "But you can."

The accusation seemed to balloon in the lofty space, bounce off the marble staircase, then thud into the wood parquet.

"When Vicki arrives," I continued, trying to repress the urge to hyperventilate. "I think she'll explain she left the jewelry box here in Black Pine and never called the Montecito police nor charged Giulio. You stole it. You're the professional thief, my Suspect X."

"I'm sorry I had to come out here and arrest your friend," said Carter. "You're very emotional. You wanted to clear him, but you couldn't."

"Empty your pockets. I bet you've got my Wallis Simpson ring."

"If I empty my pockets, will you drop this?"

My cheeks burned. I nodded. I'd grown from confrontation to accusation. My blood felt volcanic. My stomach had crawled into my mouth to hide from the lava flow that churned below. Finger-pointing didn't suit me. Especially finger-pointing at law enforcement.

We watched silently while Carter pulled out his badge, wallet, keys, and phone. He turned out his pockets. A penny fell to the floor, rolled, and stopped at my feet.

"Can you get arrested for accusing a cop?" Rhonda murmured to Tiffany.

"Look at the script left in Giulio's safe," my voice rose to levels of hysteria. "*Le Cercle Rouge* is a jewelry heist done by ex-cons and a crooked cop. Come on! Leaving that script in the safe appears to point toward

Giulio's resentment of Vicki, but it's really pointing at the crooked cop."

"Why would a crooked cop leave a clue about himself?" said Eddy. "I'm not getting it."

"It's a professional thief's idea of a joke."

"Why wouldn't he just steal it?" Eddy peered at our group through his oversized frames, not looking a bit confused. "Why is he going to make jokes that might get him arrested?"

"Shut up, Eddy," I croaked.

"Back to lockup." Ian steered Giulio toward the door. "I'm sorry it didn't work out, Maizie."

"I'm innocent," said Giulio. "How can you put an innocent man away?"

"I'm not putting you away. That's for a jury to decide. Anyway, this isn't my case. It's Montecito's. I gave Maizie a chance. She really thought the ring was stolen."

"How is this America? You aren't supposed to do the guilty until proven innocent."

"I wouldn't worry too much, Giulio." Carter opened the door. "You're rich and famous. Your kind always ends up sunny side up."

Carter strolled through the door. Heather, Eddy, and Irene followed him out.

"Sorry it didn't work." Rhonda handed me the tiara. "I'm giving this back in front of a cop, so I don't get accused of stealing it."

"That's not how I said you should put it," muttered Tiffany and shoved Rhonda out the door.

"I guess I should put this in the safe." I sighed at the tiara, then looked at Ian. "How much time do we have?"

"Carter's flight is tonight. He'll leave for Atlanta soon," said Ian. "If it makes you feel any better, even if it didn't work as you planned, I admire your gumption."

Gumption didn't seem to do me much good. "I'm

sorry about this, Giulio. But don't worry, I won't give up."

"No matter what they say, you are a good friend, Maizie." Giulio grabbed his stomach. "A good friend who is bad for my digestion."

"Come on." Ian opened the door and ushered Giulio outside.

"I'm sorry." Nash pulled me into a hug. "That must have been hard to do."

"I'm getting used to the humiliation, I guess. Isn't the mocking and embarrassment worth doing what's right?" I grimaced. "There is a thief, and it's not Giulio. Why does it have to be so hard to prove?"

TWENTY

#AKICKINTHEFAMILYJEWELS

I'D THOUGHT I still had a few aces up my sleeve. Unfortunately, I'd worn a tank top.

After saying goodbye to Nash, I headed up the back stairs with the tiara. On the landing, I checked the hall leading to the guest room wing. I half-expected Eddy or Irene to show, returning to get her things. I didn't trust either one. I should've changed the security or the door locks, not just the safe.

The guest hall was empty. I continued toward Vicki's wing. In Vicki's dressing room, I saw the door to the panic room still stood open as I'd left it. However, the safe was closed and locked.

A slight creak broke the stillness. Possibly the old home's stirring, but I knew someone was in the house. I was expecting him. I stuffed the tiara into a sock drawer and slid behind a lower rack of dark-colored slacks, mostly hidden by the island of drawers.

I didn't have to wait long. His shoes made no sound on the wood, but I had a view between hangers. Carter entered the panic room and turned toward the command center. I slid out, rushed to the outer control panel, and hit the silent panic button. He whirled around, then padded toward me. I stepped into the doorway, blocking his escape.

In a moment, the door would lock him inside until

the police arrived. I had even thought to change the security code. My plan had worked. But I still needed to buy time and distract him from the blinking panel that hadn't accepted his code.

"You shouldn't have come back. You would've gotten away."

"I couldn't resist." Carter grinned.

"I thought the Wallis Simpson ring would tempt you."

"If I had taken it, would I hide it in my pocket?"

"I mean now. Why come back? It's like you want to be caught."

"That's a fallacy. Thieves don't want to be caught. However, we sometimes make bad decisions."

"Not this time?"

"I always have an escape plan." His smile exposed dimples he'd hidden beneath his gruff facade. "How did you know it was me? *The Red Circle* script?"

"No, but that came to me last night."

"I thought it ironic." He lifted a shoulder. "Amusingly ironic."

"The first time I met you, I noticed your shoes. I can't help myself. I'm into shoes. The police detectives I know wear Rockports or black running shoes. Your black sneakers blended, but they're canvas, not leather. They also didn't have the extra cushioning cops need. I learned the hard way in my Tory Burch court shoes. Super cute, but not made for long periods of standing or walking."

"Flat feet aren't in my DNA."

"It also struck me how quiet you were. Your shoes reminded me of stage shoes. Suede soles?"

"Even rubber can make noise," he agreed. "Not stage. West Coast Swing sneakers."

Dance shoes. Call me impressed. "There was no reason for Ian to vet you with the paperwork you sent. Montecito has a Detective Carter with the same email.

He even looks somewhat like you. And he's also out of town."

"I do my research. I have digitally proficient friends."

"You mean hacking. You think yourself clever. But you purposely harmed Giulio. He'll have the arrest on his record. Why do this to him?"

"I needed a fall guy as a distraction. Tonight, Black Pine police will learn there was never a charge against Giulio. He'll walk a free man. It's nothing personal. He has money and as an actor, he'll recover professionally. It's not like he needs to reapply for real work. You both had a record. Be glad I didn't target you."

I opened my mouth and snapped it shut. "That's horrible."

"Horrible? People like Vicki and Heather have so much money they've turned collecting priceless baubles into a sport. When you can buy anything you want, only the things you can't buy become interesting."

"You're stealing to punish the rich? Like Robin Hood?"

"No, I keep the money. I get paid well to obtain these objects." He smiled. "I also enjoy a challenge. I just don't feel sorry for those I plunder."

"But I don't have money."

"That's why I didn't steal your ring. I don't have many scruples, but I do draw a line at a bank balance." He opened his jacket, displaying a wine bottle poking from a deep pocket. "I'll enjoy this."

"The Yul Brynner estate wine? You're going to drink it?"

"Hardly." He chuckled. "I was surprised to find I like you. Too bad. So how do you want to do this? I abhor violence. However, I'd hate an arrest even more. And I have a plane to catch."

TWENTY-ONE
#PLANSLAM

CARTER LUNGED. I angled my shoulder toward him and leaned, ready to push back. He side-stepped. I teetered forward, and he rammed his elbow into my side. I doubled over and he shoved. My tailbone hit the ground. The door swung shut and locked. With me inside.

He had impeccable timing.

I did not. Even after years of Kevin's kung fu training. Stage kung fu training.

Hopping up, I peered at the video monitor. Carter grinned, mouthed "sorry," and dashed off.

Shizzles.

Convinced I could trap him, I'd planned to humiliate myself with a (not false) accusation to tempt him back to the safe for the Wallis Simpson ring. I'd even disabled the panic room phone earlier when I changed the password codes. I thought I could chat up Carter long enough to lock him inside the panic room.

Not lock myself up.

No worries. I'd just wait until the police let me out. They'd been alerted with the silent panic button.

My neck felt clammy. I flapped my t-shirt and forced my brain to forget about the comfortable yet inescapable holding cell. I paced to the safe and back. It hit me.

My plan hadn't worked. This wasn't over.

And I couldn't do anything because I was trapped.

WHEN THE PANIC room door swung open (finally), I ran through the dressing room and smacked into Ian.

"Are you okay? Why are you wet?"

"Never mind that." I gave him a quick explanation of my encounter with Carter. "Did you get him?"

"No. The house is empty. He got away." His lips pressed into a grim line. "I positioned us at all the exits, then went room-by-room through the house. That's what took so long. I'll get an APB out. I know you'd suspected Carter, but you should have told me your whole plan. I feel cheated after going to the trouble of releasing Giulio temporarily."

"Carter would have gotten suspicious if you'd had multiple police cars pull up during my summation."

"More importantly, I wouldn't have allowed it."

"I figured public humiliation was more convincing. I've done it so much lately, I thought to use it to my advantage." I grabbed Ian's arm. "That being said, please trust me. I know where he went. To collect his spoils."

"What do you mean?"

"Carter told me he gets paid to obtain objects. He's not going to fence the necklace and Marilyn box. Although he did steal some jewelry and wine from Vicki." I scowled. "I had plenty of time to check while waiting."

"Where's Carter going?"

"Heather Holliday's. To return the necklace and give her the Marilyn box. Possibly, Carter had the skills to slip the necklace from Heather's neck, but he didn't have to. She gave it to him and staged the robbery. She wanted Vicki's jewelry box. Maybe to get back at Vicki, but also for her collection of celebrity jewelry."

I waited while Ian radioed his team. "There's a patrol car in that neighborhood," he said. "I've got it headed to her house. My guys will continue searching, but I sent another unit to Ms. Holliday's."

"It was brilliant. As an out-of-town cop, Carter could keep the evidence on him until the end. Heather might have gotten Eddy to help. Irene could have easily stolen the box while Vicki was in Patagonia. You need to pick up all three." I rubbed my hands together. "Another denouement. I never did two in one episode before."

"Sorry, Maizie." Ian placed a hand on my shoulder. "This time, I'll do the denouement. In separate interrogation rooms. At the police station. You're off the case."

TWENTY-TWO
#GIRL'SBESTFRIEND

THE FOLLOWING DAY, Vicki still hadn't returned from vacation. But Annie did. Therefore, I returned to storage unit surveillance. Nash returned with me. For fun. In my book, all's well that ends in the cab of a pickup.

As long as it's Nash's pickup, that is.

"It's too bad Carter got away, but at least Heather Holliday is getting what's coming to her."

"Eddy and Irene, too." Nash laid down his binoculars and faced me. "Ian said they turned on each other easily. I bet you spooked them when you accused Carter. They must have been sweating bullets, waiting to see if he had that ring."

"Humiliation really seems to work for me. Much better than confrontation."

"What would have happened if he'd had that ring in his pocket?"

"It would have been sweet." I smiled, imagining it. "And a lot less sweaty."

Nash reached into his pocket. "Like this?"

He opened his fist. On his palm lay three slender, interlaced silver bands.

I sucked in air and almost choked. "What. Is. That?"

"Not priceless. Or even expensive. It's…"

"A Russian wedding ring?" I clasped my hands to my heart.

"A fidget ring." Nash's dimple disappeared and his cheeks reddened. "Russian wedding ring? Were you expecting—"

"Expecting? No, I'm not expecting anything. You heard wrong. Of course, it's a fidget ring because I... fidget."

"I thought it would help you think. I pace and you..."

"Eat donuts?" I glared at him.

"Not what I was going to say." He closed his fist and shoved it into his pocket. "Sorry, I'm not good at this. I thought it'd be cute since you solved your first jewelry larceny."

"It is cute." I yanked on his arm. "Please. I love it."

"You love jewels." Nash sighed and opened his hand. "I can't afford jewels."

"I have jewels. Gift jewels. I don't need jewels. I do need something to help me think." I slid on the ring and displayed my right hand. Then gave him my best *Maxim* cover smile with a sultry wink. "How's it look?"

"I don't know about the ring, but you look gorgeous, as usual." His dimple reappeared. "How about I give you something to think about to make that ring spin?"

"Great idea." I leaned toward him. "But make my head spin instead?"

"Miss Albright, I thought you'd never ask."

The End.
(But not really. 21 GUNS comes next!)

A NOTE TO MY READERS

FIRST, I must apologize to my readers for giving you a book out of order. Here's what happened...

I was writing *19 Criminals* (Maizie #8) when the wonderfully talented (and super sweet) Tonya Kappes asked me if I wanted to write a novella for Twisty Tales and Cozy Crimes. Of course, I said yes (who can say no to Tonya? I love me some Tonya!).

I faced a five-month deadline and a dilemma — I had no novella on the back burner. Because I was deep in a Maizie, I went with Maizie. I came up with an idea for a Maizie and Giulio cat burglar prequel story (I love cat burglars and I don't like murdering people in 30,000 words or less). With that story in mind, I sat down to write.

And Nash turned up in the first scene.

I thought, "Okay Nash, obviously you don't want to leave Maizie alone with Giulio. How about the two of you sit in the cozy truck cab doing surveillance while she relates her first case that took place back in California before she was arrested and shipped off to Georgia?" I'd write the story in flashback, which would be a fun challenge...

And then Nash drove Maizie to the scene of the crime.

This fictional man was not letting me write my prequel.

I was in a time crunch. Get the story written in four months to get it to my editor with plenty of time to spare. Write it between the day job, a voracious volleyball schedule (I don't play, the second daughter does), and a college student coming home for the summer.

A few chapters in, I gave up. Not only did Nash reoccur in scenes, Tiffany and Rhonda had slipped into the story as well. Although Tiffany and Rhonda don't really slip — more like party crashed their way in.

I'd already had 20 Carats as the title name after 19 Criminals. 20 was going to have to be a novella. However, 20 Carats wouldn't release in stores until October 2023. I hoped 19 would release before then, but ever since Covid wiped out my freelance jobs and turned my husband's career upside down, my writing life has not been the same. As it turned out, 20 would release in stores before 19.

How embarrassing.

I fretted about this for four months and finally gave up when I got my notes back from my editor on the Maizie and Nash interplay. "A real Nick & Nora exchange," she'd said.

I love Nick and Nora. I hadn't thought about them while writing, but I guess Nash did. (*Clue*, the movie, kept coming to mind during my edits…)

Nash is forgiven.

I hope you enjoy it, too!

Happy reading,

Larissa

P.S. Don't forget to grab a free Finley Goodhart short story at LarissaReinhart.com with my VIP Readers signup!

LARISSA'S GIFT TO YOU!

THE PIG'N A POKE

A Finley Goodhart Crime Caper prequel

When a winter storm traps ex-con Finley at the Pig'N a Poke roadhouse, she finds her criminal past useful in solving a murder.

Free for my VIP Readers!

Join Larissa's email group by tapping the VIP Reader box at the top of her website at LarissaReinhart.com. The VIP Reader email is where she shares exclusive content, news, and giveaways. You'll receive *The Pig'N A Poke* as a gift in your first email.

Note: Larissa will not share your email address and you can unsubscribe at any time.

19 CRIMINALS

MAIZIE ALBRIGHT STAR DETECTIVE 8

IS IT CONSIDERED STALKING YOUR BOYFRIEND IF HE'S INVOLVED IN YOUR MURDER INVESTIGATION? (ASKING FOR A FRIEND)

Turner & Hooch meets *Mr. and Mrs. Smith* in the eighth book of the *Wall Street Journal* best-selling Maizie Albright Star Detective series. For fans of rom-com mysteries who like quirky characters, funny fast-paced plots, and amateur sleuthing heroines who earnestly agonize over (but not between) murder and marriage.

———

Nominated For 2025 Georgia Author of the Year, Best Romance
2025 Silver Falchion Judge's Pick - Best Cozy Mystery

"Fans of humorous mysteries like Janet Evanovich's Stephanie Plum, and Elle Cosimano's Finlay Donovan should pick up this series. We all need some fun in our reading lives!"

SARAH CAN'T STOP READING

 # WannabeMrsSmith Ex-celebrity and current (assistant) private investigator Maizie Albright finds her already strange life has become even odder. Her new partner is two hundred pounds and canine. And her ex-partner/still-boyfriend is on the wrong side of her infidelity case.

It's *Spy vs. Spy* — or rather, Detective vs. Detective — when Maizie and Nash realize they're both tailing the same subject for very different reasons. Can Maizie out-investigate Nash to learn the secrets he's probing into at her father's company? Secrets she fears are much darker (and stinkier) than the secret DeerNose formula. Secrets possibly related to old rivalries and a recent murder.

Her relationship is on the line, but it's more than her heart at stake. Her career rests on this case. And there's a killer at large. One who will do anything to keep dark secrets from getting dragged into the light.

Order 19 Criminals today and find out why readers call the Maizie Albright series "tremendously entertaining" and "a great combination of mystery, comedy, and a little romance."

"The banter between Maizie and her besties is witty and always a delight, and the plot moves swiftly along and proves to be extremely grounded and compelling."

CYNTHIA CHOW, *KINGS RIVER LIFE MAGAZINE*

21 GUNS

MAIZIE ALBRIGHT STAR DETECTIVE 10

A MAGIC GUN, A CURSED MOVIE SET, AND A MYSTERIOUS DEATH. ALL TRICKS AND NO TREATS FOR MAIZIE ALBRIGHT

It's the ex-celebrity and wannabe detective's tenth case in *Wall Street Journal* bestselling author Larissa Reinhart's Maizie Albright Star Detective series. For fans of rom-com mysteries who like an extra "ha" with their "Aha." An extra *"Kiss Kiss"* with their *"Bang Bang."* And an extra *Shot in the Dark* with their tall and handsome.

#CursedDetective In a spine-tingling case of Clue meets Scream, former actress Maizie Albright is about to learn that some Hollywood nightmares don't need special effects. When a real gun plays peek-a-boo with the prop weapons on a horror movie set, horror producer Michael Meyers (not that one, the other one) hires Maizie and her PI mentor Nash to track it down.

The plot thickens faster than fake blood, when a prop assistant's accident turns out to be the premiere of a murderer's masterpiece. As the body count rises and the production deadline looms, Maizie and Nash must solve the case before the killer decides it's time for their curtain call.

"This series is always good for a little suspense; plenty of twists and turns to keep you guessing."

SAMANTHA, COZY TEA COTTAGE

PORTRAIT OF A DEAD GUY

A CHERRY TUCKER MYSTERY BOOK 1

"LAUGH-OUT-LOUD FUNNY AND AS SOUTHERN AS SWEET TEA AND CHEESE GRITS"

From Wall Street Journal bestselling author, Larissa Reinhart. The first in the sassy and Southern Cherry Tucker cozy mystery series, a Woman's World Magazine 2018 book club pick, Daphne Du Maurier finalist, The Emily finalist, Dixie Kane Memorial Winner, and Night Owl Review top pick.

"Reinhart is a truly talented author and this book was one of the best cozy mysteries we reviewed this year. We highly recommend this book to all lovers of mystery books."

MYSTERY TRIBUNE

In Halo, Georgia, folks know Cherry Tucker as big in mouth, small in stature, and able to sketch a portrait faster than buckshot rips from a ten gauge — but commissions are scarce. So when the well-heeled Branson family wants to memorialize their murdered son in a coffin portrait, Cherry scrambles to win their patronage from her small town rival.

As the clock ticks toward the deadline, Cherry faces more trouble than just a controversial subject. Between ex-boyfriends, her flaky family, an illegal gambling ring, and outwitting a killer on a spree, Cherry finds herself painted into a corner she'll be lucky to survive.

"An entertaining mystery full of quirky characters and solid plotting. Highly recommended for anyone who likes their mysteries strong and their mint juleps stronger!"

JENNIE BENTLEY, NEW YORK TIMES
BESTSELLING AUTHOR

"Author Reinhart dishes out shovelfuls of ribald humor and mayhem. It takes a rare talent to successfully portray a beer-and-hormone-addled artist as a sympathetic and worthy heroine, but Reinhart pulls it off with tongue-in-cheek panache."

MYSTERY SCENE MAGAZINE

"Laugh-out-loud funny and as Southern as sweet tea and cheese grits, Larissa Reinhart's masterfully crafted whodunit, Portrait of a Dead Guy, provides high-octane action with quirky, down-home characters and a trouble-magnet heroine who'll steal readers' hearts."

DEBBY GIUSTI, PUBLISHER'S
WEEKLY BESTSELLING AUTHOR

THE CUPID CAPER

FINLEY GOODHART CRIME CAPERS
BOOK 1

"SEXY, SASSY, AND SOUTHERN SUSPENSE AT ITS BEST."

From *The Wall Street Journal* best-selling author, Larissa Reinhart, the first in a Southern con-artist, romantic mystery thriller, the Finley Goodhart Crime Caper series. A 2021 Page Turner Awards winner.

"This is as fun a novel as it is moving and at times heartbreaking, never the more so when the final page comes and readers are only left wanting more."

CYNTHIA CHOW, KING'S RIVER LIFE
MAGAZINE

Ex-grifter Finley Goodhart may try to stay on the straight and narrow, but walking that thin line becomes wobbly when she believes her friend Penny was murdered. The last thing she wants is to work with her ex-partner (and ex-boyfriend), the brilliant (brilliantly frustrating) British con artist, Lex Leopold. However, when it appears Penny's demise might be related to an exclusive matchmaking service for millionaires, Fin needs Lex's help to pull a long con to get the goods on Penny.

Romance is in the air for hustlers, gangsters, and their marks. Unfortunately for Fin and Lex, infiltrating the racket doesn't make for a match made in heaven. This Valentine swindle could stop their hearts for good.

"Once again, Larissa delivers a humorous tale that shows the struggles of a determined woman who has the guts to do what must be done. Expertly written with engaging dialogue and a fast-paced read, this mystery kept me glued to the pages."

DRU ANN LOVE, EDGAR AND AGATHA AWARD-WINNING DRU'S BOOK MUSINGS

"One thing I can always count on from this author is her fabulously strong female characters. Fin doesn't disappoint and the mystery takes many twists and turns to keep a reader guessing to the very end."

BIBLIOPHILE REVIEWS

"Another great mystery by Larissa Reinhart. Con artists, murder, a cast of sinister characters, and some laughs along the way. Loved it."

TERRI L. AUSTIN, BESTSELLING AUTHOR OF THE ROSE STRICKLAND MYSTERIES

LARISSA'S SERIES

THE MAIZIE ALBRIGHT STAR DETECTIVE SERIES

15 MINUTES

16 MILLIMETERS

NC-17

A VIEW TO A CHILL

17.5 CARTRIDGES IN A PEAR TREE (novella)

18 CALIBER

18 1/2 DISGUISES

19 CRIMINALS

20 CARATS (novella)

21 GUNS

"Child star and hilarious hot mess Maizie Albright trades Hollywood for the backwoods of Georgia and pure delight ensues. Maizie's my new favorite escape from reality."

GRETCHEN ARCHER, *USA TODAY*
BESTSELLING AUTHOR OF THE
DAVIS WAY CRIME CAPER SERIES

Ex-teen TV and reality star, Maizie Albright, returns home to Black Pine, Georgia, determined to start a new career as a private investigator, modeled after her childhood starring role as *Julie Pinkerton, Teen Detective*. Unfortunately, Maizie's chosen mentor, Wyatt Nash of Nash Security Solutions, is not a willing teacher and her learning curve includes becoming her own person after spending a life under the thumb of managers, directors, and producers, particularly her stage-monster mother.

"Ms. Reinhart has struck gold with these characters and written them into a fabulous and funny mystery story. Twists and turns, romantic tension, great dialogue full of humor and fast quips, along with some Southern flair had these pages absolutely flying."

GREAT ESCAPES

———

A CHERRY TUCKER MYSTERY SERIES

"Readers who like a little small-town charm with their mysteries will enjoy Reinhart's series."

DENISE SWANSON, *NEW YORK TIMES* BESTSELLING AUTHOR OF THE *SCUMBLE RIVER MYSTERIES*

A CHRISTMAS QUICK SKETCH (prequel)

PORTRAIT OF A DEAD GUY

STILL LIFE IN BRUNSWICK STEW

HIJACK IN ABSTRACT

THE VIGILANTE VIGNETTE

DEATH IN PERSPECTIVE

THE BODY IN THE LANDSCAPE

A VIEW TO A CHILL

A COMPOSITION IN MURDER

A MOTHERLODE OF TROUBLE (novella with Carolyn Haines' Trouble the Cat Detective)

Meet Cherry Tucker, big in mouth, small in stature, and able to sketch a portrait faster than kudzu climbs telephone poles! The Cherry Tucker Mystery series (Henery Press) begins with Portrait of a Dead Guy, a 2012 Daphne du Maurier finalist, a 2012 The Emily finalist, a 2011 Dixie Kane Memorial winner, and a Woman's World Magazine book club pick for 2018!

"An entertaining mystery full of quirky characters and solid plotting… Highly recommended for anyone who likes their mysteries strong and their mint juleps stronger!"

JENNIE BENTLEY, NEW YORK TIMES BESTSELLING AUTHOR OF *FLIPPED OUT*

———

FINLEY GOODHART CRIME CAPERS

"As fun as it is moving and at times heart-breaking, never the more so when the final page comes and readers are only left wanting more."

CYNTHIA CHOW, *KING'S RIVER LIFE MAGAZINE*

THE PIG'N A POKE (prequel, short story)

THE CUPID CAPER

THE PONY PREDICAMENT (coming soon!)

THE HEIR AFFAIR (coming soon!)

Ex-con Finley Goodhart finds her criminal past – and criminal ex-boyfriend – useful in catching crooks. Can she make up for her past by helping victims double-cross their swindler? More importantly, can she convince Lex that going straight is the best (and most challenging) hustle of all?

"Faced paced, bold, heartbreaking, this book has it all. It takes us deep into the world of hustlers, cons and dirty business. Highly recommended for lovers of mystery and thrillers."

ABOUT THE AUTHOR

Wall Street Journal bestselling and international award-winning author, Larissa Reinhart writes humorous mysteries and romantic comedies including the critically acclaimed Maizie Albright Star Detective, Cherry Tucker Mystery, and Finley Goodhart Crime Caper series. Her works have been chosen as book club picks by *Woman's World Magazine* and *Hot Mystery Reviews*.

Larissa's family and dog, Biscuit, had been living in Japan, but once again call Georgia home. See them on HGTV's *House Hunters International* "Living for the Weekend in Nagoya" episode. Visit her website —LarissaReinhart.com — join her VIP Readers Group, and get a free short Finley Goodhart story.

www.ingramcontent.com/pod-product-compliance
Lightning Source LLC
Chambersburg PA
CBHW010347220726
48290CB00016B/2669